A LITTLE DECORUM, FOR ONCE

A

LITTLE DECORUM, FOR ONCE

▼

W. M. Spackman

ALFRED A. KNOPF
New York 1985

THIS IS A BORZOI BOOK
PUBLISHED BY ALFRED A. KNOPF, INC.

Library of Congress Cataloging in Publication Data
Spackman, W. M. (William Mode)
A little decorum, for once.
1. Title.
PS3569.P3L5   1985   813'.54   85-40124
ISBN 0-394-54722-5

Short passages have appeared in slightly different form
in *Town & Country* and in *Parnassus*.

Manufactured in the United States of America

FIRST EDITION

to
Harriet Newell

and to
Alice Quinn

and, always, to
Laurice

On a dit, l'an passé, que j'imitais Byron.
Vous qui me connaissez, vous savez bien que non.

A LITTLE DECORUM, FOR ONCE

1

From the cardiac care he responsibly assured his family and friends could hardly be his deathbed ("At a still marauding sixty-plus? *god* no!") a novelist named Scrope Townshend rang up his many-times-past love Laura Tench-Fenton and said angel look: not to be startled, but how about his doing that glossy high-fashion magazine of hers a civilized couple of thousand words on adultery?—though clearly, in the circumstances, this would take any editor aback.

So, naturally, "But Scrope *sweetie* what is this!" she cried at him, as in tenderest shock and concern. "I mean of *all* possible mad— Oh my dear of course *how* kind to offer it to me I know, but just when we've all been utterly ill worrying weren't you perhaps even dying my old darling?—and *that* topic?" she rebuked him with brisk editorial impatience. "My dear man for *my* readers? heavens!" and in fact this sort of thing it happened they had many times before disingenuously wrangled over, even as often their long once-upon-a-time as bed together.

So he was amused. Woman's happiest birthright and perquisite not for her readers?—dear god who were this sad circulation of hers, faithful wives or something?

"But you're in intensive *care!*" she cried, as if the man were unhinged.

Any better place to waste time and genius on a thinkpiece in? —tell him what else do, lying there!—regretting his regrettable past with he hoped the required piety, in particular—

" 'Piety' oh *listen* to you!"

—in particular deploring all the passed-up opportunities he'd been too much of a gent, or ah sometimes just too dazzled, to understand this or that lovely apparition was offering him.

"Oh how *can* you be so light-minded in practically Scrope the shadow of death aren't you still?" she denounced him, as if in grief for him already. " 'A civilized couple of thous—' And when it's not a *week* since that ambulance hurtled you writhing and gasping through the night to thank God emergency? so bludgeoned and beaten by that awful thudding pain it took no fewer than *four* injections of morphine, the absolute Sibylla said limit they dared give you, even to begin the— Oh you madden me, sweetie who wouldn't you madden!"

Been a bit, yes, he'd concede, like being beaten to pulp by jack-hammers. But by now he'd completely—

"And when you groggily asked that duty doctor working on you what kind of heart attack was it you were having, Sibylla told me this man—who *knew!*—this man said, 'The bad kind,' do you deny it? And when at last she went home hopeless and weeping because they didn't even feel they could encourage the sweet darling her father would last the night, she lay there praying and *praying* when practically she doesn't believe in God d'you think in the slightest!"

He said but—

"And even *she* it wasn't till yesterday was allowed to visit you for more than five minutes at a time once an hour! And in *your* condition you ring me up about Heaven knows what wicked sardonic upsetting article you pretend to think I'd for one instant— 'Adultery'! when you've just for all we know been no more than the next heartbeat from *death?*" she upbraided him, in a voice of tears.

So, after a moment, he said, mildly, well God bless. And what a lovely tirade.

Then, for another moment, slightly longer, they were silent. As, perhaps, each admitting.

But then, "No but my elegant creature look," he went back, "the thing's already written, is why, is all. I did it weeks ago. For *Vanity Fair*. Was asked to. Wonderful title, too—'Your Neighbor's Wife, Her Acquisition and Care.' In other words the social decencies of the thing, d'ye see: La Rochefoucauld stuff. Decorum, Laura, dammit! So calm down. Only now this morning here's a letter regretting changing their collective minds about running it! So all I get—"

"The hospital lets you have *mail?*"

"Good god why not!—something the matter with me? So now, d'you see, all I'm getting's a kill-fee for the thing—*me*, Laura! Well, is the stuff just to be scrapped, for God's sweet sake? So I naturally thought all right then, change the slant, nothing easier *or* simpler—change the man-about-town pretexts and fatuities into women's and there you are. Or change into both's, why not —I can for instance see a very handsome layout with a subhead added: 'Your Neighbor's Wife, Her Acquisition and Care (And What She Can Do To Help).' Can you resist it? How can you resist it! And I'll have it in your hands in forty-eight hours."

Mrs. Tench-Fenton demanded, as of a child, was he *totally* unteachable? Or just didn't he listen!

But here was dear god an activity everybody could enjoy! *Did* enjoy! Most of those faithful-wife readers of hers included!

Did he expect her to *purvey* his kind of scoffing irresponsible misbehavior?—indeed *not*!

What was this 'misbehavior'?—when everybody believed in a given way of acting, that way became accepted comportment— was normal *be*havior, not *mis*. What was the matter with her?— been a faithful wife at one misguided period herself hadn't she? so she knew what happens!

"And anyhow dammit," he ran smoothly on, forestalling her, "why not consider running the thing with a matching piece by a woman on the facing page, making sense of the feminine side of the pastime? Or the feminist side even, good god why not—one of those outraged fuming confutations they do so beautifully, demolishing me!"

She said, sounding amused, she supposed what he meant was— Well in particular who had he thought of suggesting to *her* might do this did he mean?

Why should he have thought of anybody. Be up to her, he'd've thought. Only thing was, they wouldn't want some bed-room freudiologist writing it, tone wrong into the bargain! What was called for was blandness. Even in a high-style rebuttal. Why, anybody'd do; couldn't say he'd thought of anybody in particular. Of course if she—

"You haven't *any* alluring little thing you're as usual after in mind, for me to help you with?"

" 'After'!—how d'ye mean, 'after'?"

"What would anybody mean! So then who?"

So he said, in an honest voice, that in point of fact it had occurred to him that Sibylla's friend Amy Hallam did somewhat that *sort* of short stories—she might try her hand at it. But *damned* if he was 'after' her or anything like it!—his own daughter's college roommate?

Mrs. Tench-Fenton was silent.

"Anyhow Laura you know the child already, you ran a story of hers a year or so ago. Very gifted young woman. And the thing is, she'd do you a nice sexy *either* feminine or feminist job, whichever. Editorially speaking ideal, in short. What's the matter, you don't think so?"

Still she was silent.

So naturally he laughed at her. "You're not going to maintain the young woman's unqualified to write about adultery because she's not married good god?"

"Well she isn't is she? She just lives with Charles Ebury! Or he with her, heavens do I know which?"

"But they—"

"And when he's so charming!"

"But what's *his*—"

"I don't even like her novels!"

"But the story you ran—"

"Was what my last year's stupid story editor—Scrope *sweetie* how can you be so perverse and unendurable! when why can't you *see* there isn't the slightest pretext I could run your impossible graceless effrontery of an article using! Print *your* idea of behavior for an even remotely— So once for all *oh will you give up* about it!" she commanded, as in an absolute fume.

So (it not mattering much anyhow) he obeyed.

And modulated smoothly into gossip. Charles Ebury had as

it happened just this morning—had he told her?—dropped by. Very kind; couldn't have been kinder. Not been allowed to see him of course, but he'd left him an amusing note: "My current in-house othersex sends her fond love too." Very amusing. But then, Charles was a wit. Except ah well, what a way for even a Classics professor to describe a delicious girl, lived-with or not. Did she suppose Amy herself—

But here, "Oh Scrope my dear I do have to ring off, I must go I must go, you *know* this endless magazine of mine, oh isn't one so helpless always!" Mrs. Tench-Fenton wailed, as in lady-like despair. "And when anyway I've only talked *this* long to make sure—for *myself*, poor darling—that you were as well again as oh thank God you obviously are, I mean disputing with me in your usual self-serving bullying chauvinist fashion about things you know to *begin* with are totally out of the question, oh you're distracting!—and when we have all been so *deeply* worried Scrope over you, oh if you loved me you'd promise you'd never argue with me about anything again ever!"

So he snorted—what was this '*if* he loved her'! What had he become to her, then, dammit, some sort of merely vestigial him? —a man who'd adored her from the first dazed moment he'd laid eyes on her, as by *god* she knew!

"Allowing you mean for the interludes? *And* intervals, sweetie! *All* those intervals!"

He demanded, with some heat, did she dammit have to affront his feelings about her with these pitiless libels? when there wasn't a heroine in his uncollected works that didn't somehow mirror her!—her dizzying moods, her follies, her flighty sophist of a heart, even that delicious fluttering she used for syntax had got into his novels, where did she think the charm came from?—in for instance scenes like What's-his-name's coming round the corner of Miranda's roommate's house, heart pounding with manly hope—

"Oh Scrope not that memorized passage *again!*"

—to the two girls 'dawdling in garden chairs by a pool, sunning their pretty legs. Miranda was singing some French song or other, clapping her palms together to beat time. She was in summer white, her sleek arms bare; her sun-flooded dark beauty—'

Mrs. Tench-Fenton said oh *really* the purposes he seemed to think women were created for! Also for her taste he had used that 'sun-flooded' of his *much* too much, in fact ever since he had thought it up, why didn't that editor he was always saying was so wonderful (as well as an angel!) call his lazy attention to it? Also anyway it had been her roommate singing too. Also all *right* if he insisted, on occasion she had indulged him, and if that struck him as light-minded what did its even *being* light-minded matter, goodness! And as if she hadn't known it herself!—imagine *any* woman's not knowing she was only doing what she was doing because she was young and giddy even while she was young and giddy doing it! So she had a *right* to worry about him, and if they'd moved him out of intensive care into a private room he still had monitors stuck all over him hadn't he?—so when Sibylla worried why shouldn't anyone who loved him worry too? oh he was detestable!

Yes, well, he said mildly, after a moment, yes the heart unit had, he'd of course concede, been something of a memento mori, how did those splendid duty nurses stand it, hour after hour? For instance in the cubicle across from his there had been this huge dying hulk of (he'd found out) a ship's captain, an enormous man, lost and wandering in delirium on top of everything else, and he kept bellowing for his lawyers.

'Lawyers'?

Well it seemed he thought he was being held captive by sea-going gangsters, in some waterfront dive! So, to escape, he kept pulling out the various tubes they had in him, nurses were lugging blood-soaked bedding out every half-hour or so; amazing! So finally they actually lashed the poor devil's wrists to the bed-rails! —except then by god what did he do but work his way round till he could tear the knots loose with his great teeth, could she imagine such a thing?

"Ah Scrope . . ."

But then, that second night, in the middle of one of those hoarse raging Achillean tantrums, suddenly there had come this, well, it was the *suddenness* of the stillness. And the rush of the nurses. To what was no longer there . . . Very *moving*, somehow. To have lain there, listening. Though why 'moving'? One's impersonal interest, as at a play? Or is it merely human decency— sympathy for the race of man. Or was it 'moved' (as at a play) in a sort of Aristotelian satisfaction at the well-constructed Sopho-clean dénouement, 'Zeus still Zeus' in fact, and the audience homeward bound, purged and edified? . . .

But "Oh sweetie now I *must* sign off," she regretted, "I must I *must*, I am enslaved to this inexorable magazine, and when you haven't even told me how is your heavenly Sibylla of a daughter."

He said need he say couldn't be sweeter?—"Comes to see me in this damn place two and three times a day."

"Yes how does she manage?"

So he said and how was that huge stepson of hers and his latest guggenheim.

"Do I ever see him, to find out?" she cried. "Though Scrope he does have a splendid I'm told poem in some quarterly, one of those tensely intellectual quarterlies I think, the *Susquehanna* is it? Quite a long poem, too. *Pages.*"

He said narrative, huh.

"No I don't think so, just more sort of—oh *you* know, more sort of what he feels about how he feels."

He said um.

"And you don't in the least care anyhow!" she told him, though then, for a wary moment, and this was perhaps mutual good manners and forgiveness, they were silent.

But she had to go.

"Because now my sweet old darling I do have to hang up on you, oh how sad always," she lamented. "Except do you never Scrope wonder a little about the pair of them, those special two of ours, together?"

He snickered bless God what an unseemly question!

"No but I mean about their being married to each *other*. Being who they are."

"What's this being who—Alec you mean yours and she mine?"

"Yes, and, well, being *married*, sweetie. Are they d'you truly think happy."

"Happy how? Way we were?"

"Well of course, but happily *married*."

"Why shouldn't they be happy? Sibylla's a lovely thing, what could any man want! And a sweet besides! And, well, Alec's this splendid huge jock of a Discobolos if you like—good god Laura in principle what more'd either of 'em want!"

"But as happy as we've been? Oh Scrope don't you ever wonder whether sometimes— Because can it be the same sort of *match*. My dear she's like you, the sweet, but who Alec's like is his father, who was *splendidly* what you called my bel homme tendency if ever anyone was!"

Her bel homme 'frailty' was the word. Never lifted a finger! Bill Basset was another of 'em. And worse!

"So you see Alec and Sibylla aren't really a sort of thing like you and me at *all*, I mean."

What she mean, 'she meant'?

"But how they feel about each other, heavens!—not like *us* can it be, surely? Because is your lovely Sibylla's temperament any more a cleave-to d'you think than yours?—and Scrope you can't *not* see how like Alec is to his father instead?"

. . . Hadn't turned out to be all that cleaved-*to*, either, she meant? Or was it 'cloven-to.'

"As who knows better than you!"

Ah, well, he said, beaux hommes. They did often turn out to be temptable-from, anyhow. Women being, upon reflection, women. His darling daughter he supposed included, never *had* got used to producing anything so delicious!

Mrs. Tench-Fenton opened her eyes at him instantly. "Do you mean about Charles Ebury?" she demanded.

"Now what's this!" he cried, as in alarm.

"Well but I understood he was helping her with this *very* it seems amusing libretto isn't he? Because *Charles* I should have thought— Well I had a fascinating talk with him at a party, about *Ovid* can you imagine? all I'd somehow thought Ovid'd written was that collection of nursery-tale myths, but Charles said his *Helen to Paris* letter is the basis for the whole genre of psychology-of-love novels from Mme. de La Fayette on. He promised to do me an article on it, what an angel, I don't wonder Sibylla's putting him to work! But surely you'd heard, didn't she tell you? Because certainly *he* could be a temptation without lifting a finger either!"

"Dammit," the father cried, as if humorously, "what kind of interlocking triangles are you trying to upset me with!"

"Well sweetie there *is* after all us! You don't feel anybody's ever going to think they're proxies for us somehow?"

"Proxies for *our* happy behavior, woman?" he demanded of her, greatly amused.

"*Now* who's unseemly!" she chanted, sounding amorous; and they hung up, snickering if only in memory.

2

Those at any rate married children of theirs, whose name was Urquhart, it happened were discussing them too, late that evening, before bed.

Or anyhow Sibylla, creaming her fashionable face at her dressing glass, was tenderly fretting about her father.

"Imagine letting a man as near death as Daddy was have a telephone! Have they no sense? How's he to rest properly, Alec? I was beside myself!"

This however her huge young husband, yawning at his image in the pier glass beyond, might well have been too sodden with sleep, by the look of him, to grasp was a concern.

"And you know how Daddy is!" she denounced him. "Now he'll wear himself out haranguing everybody he knows!"

So the man appeared to search, vacant. Though at last, ". . . nm," he came up with, swaying.

"So he's maddening!" the daughter cried lovingly. "For example when I got to the hospital this morning he was just hanging up from talking who knows how long to of all people your sweet m'ma, trying to palm off an article on her! And simply because some other editor had turned it down, well I despaired! Oh and I forgot to tell you—yesterday when he was still half-stoned and babbling I found out how the two of them first met, Alec!"

But he, lurched round, was now straggling yawning toward their bed, and mumbled only a mindless ". . . ng?" in reply.

"Well, parents, yes! But it seems it was the very first piece Daddy ever wrote for her, was how. Way back, darling; she was working for some chichi decorators' thing that isn't published now. You and I weren't even born, can you imagine? One 'theme' of this particular issue it seems was to be Tables— Are you listening to me or aren't you?" she demanded, for he was now toppling, stuporous, onto their great soft-billowing white circle of a bed, into which he now sank, spent.

She watched this, as tolerantly analyzing it.

"But what have you been doing, to be this great tedious tired hulk from, all suddenly?" she now accused him, sounding amused. "Not surely some of your time-wasting little slinks of student groupies again you've put up with!"

He made some vague disavowing sound, stretching happily, as in innocence and contentment, deep in down.

"Goodness shall I be jealous of you or something?" she laughed. "Poor catnip darling, having to fend off sophomores! As I do of course hope you of course do. No, but imagine," she went on, "Daddy said they'd not only never met but he'd never so much as heard of her when out of the blue there she was! Would he consider doing them fifteen hundred of his lovely words on for example strange hosts he had known? Or odd table-conversations. Or eccentric seating-protocols. Or of course any angle he wanted to propose himself instead, because they did so want *him* in this issue, his wit and the way he wrote his brilliant novels—oh well darling you know that coaxing caressing absolutely seducing voice of hers, as if she's Daddy said about to murmur herself into bed with you!"

The son-in-law muttered something derisive-sounding, "nole edger," it seemed.

"Oh ptah, he isn't! Anyway he certainly wasn't old *then!* Anyway if he's unteachable are you with your simpering students all that different? And Amy says Charles either! Well naturally Daddy told your m'ma how flattering, he'd be delighted to, though how about something with perhaps a bit more *his* sort of slant? Of course she breathed at him oh what a heavenly thing to suggest, without bothering to wait and hear what he was suggesting —which of course, it being Pa, was what does happen at tables: he'd do her a man and a girl meeting for lunch at Les Piérides with something in mind. So that's what it seems he did. And sent it round to her without bothering his agent, that voice of hers, goodness! Well but next *day* Alec there on his doorstep was a messenger with an enormous bouquet of bird-of-paradise flowers! —and being Pa he fell in love with her then and there, oh really darling the *seductions* of your mother!"

. . . stepmother.

"So he instantly rang her up and asked her to lunch. And, being Daddy, at Les Piérides."

Said nnnn.

"So I was wildly amused. Only then he got off onto something else. But then coming home I remembered wasn't there a magazine-editor heroine in *A Time Was Had By All?* So I looked it up. And there is; called Miranda. And the second time the hero takes her to lunch it says it's 'the second time they'd ever laid eyes on each other,' which would fit, Alec! And then the way he describes her, because listen to what I found, I marked the place, because it's absolutely—well, listen!

. . . her eyes overflowing with light at him before she'd even
sipped her Punt e Mes

—which Alec she *still* drinks now and then, and who else ever
does, goodness! Except this second restaurant was way down in
what Daddy calls 'the wilds below Canal Street' somewhere,
Cacciapuoti's did you ever hear of it? Very elegant, in the book.
Except it has an upstairs balcony out over the street but all there
is across is warehouses. Would he bother to invent that? So it
must actually have happened. Most of the places in his novels of
course haven't been there for years by our time; Daddy's geog-
raphy is sweetly archaic, is all. And then anyway it could really
have been almost any random seduced girl, you know how he is."

Her husband grunted something, it could have been dispar-
aging, into his pillow, turned now away.

"Well darling *he* feels like that about *poets!*" she laughed.
"What am I to do, between you? Each of you snorting why even
consider writing in the other's worn-out form! Oh dear I suppose
you're slighting and dismissive about novels to your adoring students too, corrupting them! No, but about your m'ma back then,
still young and volage the way who isn't—this affair with Daddy
must have been don't you suppose long before she was married to
your father? Daddy perhaps hadn't met my mother either—
darling they *can't* have been lovers with you and me in a crib in
the next room, goodness how indecorous, and they were properly
brought up, Alec!"

He had however it seemed dozed peacefully off.

"Though what era was it. Do we even know? Also they could
have taken their affair up again later couldn't they," this permissive daughter theorized. "I expect it would depend on what they'd
broken off over. She could temporarily have met someone else. Or

Daddy could've. Or whichever, but still the other one lovingly there, hoping and so on. Or one of them's getting married could have ended it for the time?"

But he it appeared slumbered on, beyond such cares.

"Oh but then Alec how exhausting, in those days! Because think!—being brought up the way they were, to be seriously responsible socially, think of the endless time-taking stealths, to protect each other's spouse's feelings!—the way in Daddy's novels it's not just unkind not to, it's inexcusable! They loved whoever they were married to *too*. Except Amy says but the first time you met a man who was going to be your lover naturally you didn't know he was going to be, so how could they start to be careful and dissembling? Only then hoh, who she met like that was *Charles!*" she mocked, but now suddenly in the glass her eyes were on her husband's slumbering image. " 'Didn't know'?—when who wouldn't *think!*" she murmured, though the sleeper did not stir. ". . . a man like Charles?"

So for a long moment then she seemed to muse, eyes lost in her own eyes in the glass once more.

But soon, "Oh well Amy does fuss about what to have her story characters feel," she went on. "And asks *me* darling! And such simple-minded questions sometimes! If one spouse is having an affair she said doesn't the other spouse sense it? And somehow show it? She said if you didn't wouldn't your husband just perhaps think you didn't care what he did? Well, imagine! Naturally I said why should the wife show she knew, heavens. She said but wouldn't a used-to-you man like a husband notice some difference?—could I for instance just go on making wifely love with you if you were sleeping with somebody so that you'd still not know I knew? I said don't be silly, men are stones. But she said

but suppose it was complicated, suppose the affair you, Alec, were
having was with somebody I see all the time, like her?"

In their great bed the husband's eyes suddenly opened.

"Naturally I said, 'Oh dear is he having?' and she said, 'Well
I adore him don't I?' And she did once have that crush. Of course
I said why ask *me!* when why not my dear pa? He's not only an
entirely practical writer he's very amusing in particular about
other writers' seduction scenes, or men writers' anyway, like Anna
weeping on that hard sofa and Vronski glumly pacing the floor—
he says what in God's name did Tolstoi conceive had gone *on* to
produce this preposterous scene! Did gens du monde of the time,
with seven or eight kilos of Second Empire clothes on, make love
on period sofas in drawing-rooms? Had Tolstoi ever tried it? And
those *tears?* . . . For any instructive particulars, Daddy says the
scene could have been written by Henry James!"

But her husband was staring at the ceiling, as if baffled.
Though even, it could have been, in dismay.

"What Amy really wanted was to know whether I felt she
could 'research' Daddy for her new story: how do men his age
feel she said about young women they have to deal with in the
ordinary course of things, for instance this Yale sociology in-
structress who's doing part of her dissertation on him. Of course
I told her *he* just seems to be amused; he calls it the 'in-house
school of sociology, who simply move in on you,' and why not.
Except Alec when the girl spends whole weekends at this au pair
field work with him?—'intensively observing' him or whatever it
is sociologists do?"

So he mumbled something. Though he had closed his eyes.

"Well the girl *is* very pretty. And she's Danish. But should
we be against her making him sociologically famous if that's what

she's doing? And I certainly can't say, 'Darling Pa should your dear famblies perhaps worry a little?'—as if *he* would get stuck with honorable intentions! But is he enough of an expert old marauder to take care of himself?—now that here's his heart? And darling I am still just a little upset over what I saw that Sunday. It was past *noon* they were still at breakfast when I dropped by! In dressing-gowns of course, but she was all rosy and tousled, and *under* her dressing-gown—well, remember that epigram of Charles's? 'Black chiffon isn't to sleep in, it's to sleep with in, a different activity altogether,' and oh Alec now he's had this dreadful setback what could happen, it's every Friday she comes down from New Haven! 'Lay Patterning in Scrope Townshend,' oh dear what *is* she writing about him!"

He said um.

But now she had finished.

"There!" she sighed, drifting to her feet. "And at his age, oh think," she mourned, and slowly crossed to stand beside their bed, gazing sadly down.

"And now there's been this frightening heart attack. And this girl. All these weekends *all* weekend at his age, Alec, like that? Au-pair-ing or not? . . ."

But he, like any son-in-law, merely sighed.

"And you don't even pretend to care! are you going to get over or aren't you?" she crooned at him, laughing. "You're a great torpid Gaelic lout, Daddy's *right* I'm wasted on you!" she cried lovingly. "Move over, or I won't even bother to wake you deliciously up!"

So after a babble of a late evening they made love as usual.

3

The ménage of Amy Hallam and Charles Ebury their friends held to be exemplary and also enduring, it being agreed that, given Charles's wary air of being put upon enough already, students languishing at his effortless good looks were merely unavoidable industrial hazard (though of course job-grade entitlement, depending), and look at Amy's behavior with him anyway: doting.

On occasion helpless, even, with docility.

As for example on this particular Sunday midmorning, Charles seigneurially still abed, "But oh *why* sweetie won't you let me just *ask* dear Scrope?" she was imploring him. "How can you *be* so mean to me!"—when simply this story she had in mind was to be about this younger girl in love with this older (maybe Scrope's age) man but how *much* older, how could Scrope's merely being asked his opinion of their age *differences* upset him, she wailed, dithering about picking up last night's discarded clothes as if distracted—she'd known him ever since Sibylla's and her freshman year at Vassar, she'd even known his last wife, and of *course* that infatuated-with-him classmate of theirs who'd caused that scandal, Scrope was as good as *family*.

So, if only as a responsible bedfellow, he considered her plight with indulgence. "Look, my blessing," he said—

"I am your out-of-my-*mind* blessing!" she cried at him. "Because Charles I could simply remind him he gave me the idea in the first place why couldn't I?—because sweetie he did, I *told* you! We were talking that evening at Sibylla and Alec's and he said he was beginning to think he knew so archaically little about our generation that how was he to write about it? so he wondered wasn't perhaps the practical solution to hire a live-in our-age model, for him to more or less round-the-clock observe, what she did (and even ask why!)—painters hire models, why shouldn't novelists? I told you I TOLD you, why don't you ever *liss*-sunn to me!!"

He said, amused, what was she clutching that armful of dirty clothes for?

She flung them at a chair.

And why didn't she come back like a lovely Sunday-morning girl to bed? In bed he could listen closer.

Anyhow dammit look—if Scrope himself thought he was an archaism, what use did she think his views about young women would be for *her* stories? Why did she suppose a man of Scrope's long and punishing experience would consider, with what *she*'d consider a proper seriousness, the emotions of her baby sister's generation?—Scrope couldn't have been the standard thy-bra-and-bikini-they-comfort-me type even in college, and *now* he'd as good as persuaded himself he treated women as Reciprocal Beings, he even boasted he was one of the few dozen heterosexual American males the census had found who did!

So she brooded at him.

And finally, "Well what I *didn't* tell you," she seemed to decide to confess, "is he said why didn't I leave you for a couple of weeks and move chastely in to instruct him! So, well, *goodness*, but so anyway I told him oh how flattering, was I really all young American womanhood for him? but, well, I had only these two modest talents, I said I write what Charles says my genre is and I make love with him on demand, but a *third* career? heavens!— even temporarily, no matter how clearly glamorous, so *why* do you keep saying it would 'upset' him to ask, he is sort of an old monster but he's sweet, oh Charles *tell* me!" she besought him. "Am I your very dearest frantic-over-decisions sweetie or amn't I!"

So (since she was) he replied as a decent sense of stewardship called for: hadn't it occurred to her, given Scrope's noble age, that her questions might strike the man as an inquiry as to his— call it his performance she was having the effrontery to be engaged in?—and how, he said blandly, was she going to dissemble *that*, face to face!

So she stared at him. And presently mumbled, ". . . oh."

And ah, dammit, in any case, he said, laughing, he hardly saw Scrope, of all people, ravening off after some babbling little creature only a feeling of responsibility for the species could make him rest his eyes on twice. How about coming back to bed why not. And unfuss.

She said, ". . . But he writes about them."

What if he did, she coming or wasn't she?

So she dropped onto the bed beside him, if mistrustfully.

He said look, he himself taught for example sophomores, so in line of duty he was metaphorically leered at five days a week. But what possible cross-cultural correlations did that imply? *Or* serious undertakings!

"Are you looking sort of your honest-as-daylight look at me again?" she cried, and sat up.

He said, laughing at her, was he not to impart his cultural level to this or that hoping college child? and lovingly pulled her down again.

"Don't *scoff!*" she rebuked him, and resisted. "I get very uncertain about you when you look honest, it's perfectly disgrace— Charles *no!*"

But how could so adorable a bosom become so impervious to his adoring it, when a mere hour ago—

"That was *then!* and when I spoil you you get so spoiled, and anyway," she said, and left him, in fact going back to the chairful of clothes she began sorting them, "we're discussing Scrope. Do you think he *is* in a way fascinating? Except in a way he's also like somebody-you-don't-know-very-well's great-uncle! who may I mean pounce? So he's socially confusing, one feels one ought to see him as just one more old-fashioned— Did they really call them 'libertines'?"

He said 'rakes,' even.

"But then I suppose he *is* isn't he. Only somehow he isn't! Or is it he just seems he isn't but you feel is. Because every now and then there's this sort of glimpse of how he must once have been, I mean I can perfectly *see* girls' thinking of bed about him back then, so therefore now I keep feeling I have to be not just unencouraging but absolutely unfeminine against all my instincts and responses, to save him from misinterpreting and its being sad. Oh dear. Because suppose. For how old is he actually. But then even supposing! Or d'you think. I mean if only because how would one make sure, in advance, whether in bed one mightn't have to— Oh dear, how do you say it! Only now here's this Sibylla says *sexy* Yale researcher weekends, and isn't she some sort of evidence? And don't *snicker!*—she dropped in on her father two or three Sundays ago and they looked practically she said just out of bed! One of which she says *is* double."

Man of sense; just decided on an *all*-categories model; why not! Nothing for Sibylla to worry about.

"But sweetie she's a sociologist! How could that be a *Scrope* model? And it's she observing *him*, not he her! And also she's Danish!"

He said exotic, yes. Unexpected amenities, Yale's! Of course there was that widespread intellectual fatuity at Yale to be compensated for—poor devils, you'd suppose they were refugees from the Cinquième Arrondissement if they didn't keep gabbling as if they'd brought the Arrondissement with them. So perhaps they did need these exotic solaces!

"Well except when Sibylla told me about finding this girl with her father like that, something in the way she— Sweetie it was almost as if she didn't want to tell me! But we tell each other everything! We've never been strange with each other in our lives, but here, it was as if she was being specially confiding, to cover not actually feeling confiding at all! You don't suppose there can have been something we've upset them about, Alec and Sibylla? Or has there been something she feels guilty about toward *us*. Though what? You *have* been helping her with that libretto she's writing for the League, d'you suppose it could be she's feeling apologetic about taking up your time, goodness should I have let you?"

He said, smiling, ecce novum crimen!

She was silent.

Ovid, he explained, amiably. Standard masculine disclaimer. Ergo ego sufficiam reus in nova crimina semper?—'what've I done now!' and so forth.

But she said, "But sweetie when I think about the way *I* felt practically seduced by you even before I began to think about you, why shouldn't I wonder mightn't she be starting to feel that way too? And you needn't look astonished!—don't you really sort of think, to *yourself*, you could probably seduce nearly any girl you wanted to? Oh dear do I have to marry you to keep you virtuous?"

He said dear god why not!

"But I don't think I want to! I don't want anything to keep you faithful to me but *me!*"

What vanity! he said.

"Oh well," she said, and seemed to brood. Though whether in sadness or resentment who could say.

But at last, "Oh well never *mind*," she told him. "But whichever way Scrope feels about this Yale girl, sweetie it is a *relationship* isn't it?—so how can he not have *some* opinions about their age difference. So why can't I research how he sees *himself* in it, older-man-wise, for my story? And don't say I'll tire him and make his heart worse—he can't be all that ill, his *dying's* not what Sibylla's worried over. Oh Charles can't you *see* I need to be told? I won't upset him, I *won't!*—so don't be so mean!"

And so forth and so on, till eventually she came back to bed to argue.

4

As it happened, when Sibylla had paid that morning's visit to her father he looked so much better that she sat on his bed to kiss him.

He was touched. Even mumbled a 'darling girl' in old-fashioned embarrassment.

In fact picked up her hand and kissed it.

(Which when he let it go she patted him with.)

"Well you are a sweet."

"Well so are you."

They smiled at each other.

"And looking so much better," she told him, and sat on his bedside chair.

"Ah, at any rate," he said cheerfully, "some punctual nurse isn't whisking in with her needle every couple of hours to shoot me in the small-clothes."

"Poor love."

"Not that it isn't you know fascinating stuff. At one point I distinctly remember seeing my sheets had turned into blue-green plastic—anise-flavored, too, can you imagine? So naturally I rose up and by god shed the things—tubes and attachments with them, in one grand crash. Of course the nurses were on me like whippets on a hare, and back I was indulgently put."

"Well and also, pet, when you were babbling you were hilarious. After my five minutes I'd go out into the waiting-room *convulsed*. All the poor hopeless waiting families were affronted by me!"

"Dear god I should think so!—father hovering between life and death, and she's *giggling!*"

"Except darling Daddy it *was* awful."

"Yes. Well. Chest pains. Yes. Still, elements of comedy. Huge dying man across from me ripping his tubes out, nurses just interestedly *watching* the process on their screen! But then rushing in just as he'd got the last one out, cooing 'Oh Mr. Thorgrimmsdatter what are you *doing* to yourself!' with the sweetest womanly indulgence and concern."

"Ah but darling didn't you say he died?"

"So at least God took him you mean seriously? Which reminds me—this very pretty girl parson dropped by last evening after you'd left. Or was she a deaconess? anyway she was from 'round the corner,' she said, St. Beekman the Well-Fixed or some such splendid shrine. Extraordinary visitation! I gather the principle is, one may be worried about the relevant theological data— the Afterlife after life, what's the ecology like and so on. So they come helpfully round, and we must feel free to inquire."

"Oh dear."

"What d'ye mean, 'oh dear'! I was a perfect gent—told her thank'ee, yes, but I'd read Dante, anyhow the *Inferno*, which I assumed was what mattered to the generality of the uneasy, but *god* what a delicious minister of hope might I say she was?—was she here to seduce me with doctrine as well as instruct me?"

"Pa *darling!*"

"Well in point of fact I suppose yes, I was a little stoned from the evening needle, still I thanked her politely enough, for either form of ministry—as thoughtful I told her as it was kind; but I said God's behavior toward us here on earth ('donde usciremo a riveder le stelle,' I remember quoting) hardly made a life with Him in Heaven something to look forward to. Did she know that devastating line of Istrati's?—'Tant de besoins, tant de désirs, tant de tumulte, et si peu d'éternité! Seigneur, pourquoi si maladroit avec Ton chef d'œuvre?' But it turned out she didn't understand French. Lovely girl, not a brain in her body."

"Oh *Pa!*" she mourned. "How can you behave that way!—and when you have such lovely manners!"

"Interrupting my writing with her damn' benisons call for anything as civilized as manners?"

But at this, "But darling, *writing?*" she cried, as in alarm. "Goodness, should you be? Tiring yourself?"

She have him just lie there going docilely nuts? What'd got into his women?—her lovely mother-in-law'd even been fussing about his being allowed mail! And in any case he'd been fiddling not writing: subconscious churning out its customary false starts, actually, for the most part. Would she like to hear the cockeyed first thing it had come up with this morning? he snickered, pulling his clipboard from under his pillow—though God knew who it was supposed to sound like, some halfwit recommending himself for cohabitation, or what?

I awake with the lark, genially. At breakfast I am cheerful, affectionate, gynæcotropic, and an informative talker.

Where did this kind of claptrap come from!

I breakfast on kippers and buttered eggs, on kedgeree and Canadian bacon, my fulminating disapprobation of my era at the service of mankind. My glance is mild.

"Well darling he eats rather like you, whoever!"

"Ah well I throw away nine-tenths of the deathless stuff I write anyhow, what's another nineteen-twentieths. Death, by the way (did I tell you?), as a by-product of this run-around of mine with eternity, turns out to be something I'm not alarmed by, *very* surprising! Simply the pain was so appalling that what was death! —and then, once they'd numbed the pain, I was past being frightened by anything as trivial as dying, just lay there sort of courteously interested in all those emergency people working on me with such frantic concentration. I thought, 'Be damned, must be in pretty bad shape, what d'you know!' so then of course I thought about Internal Revenue."

"Yes Daddy you said."

"Well how *do* you protect intangibles like future royalties from estate tax! But then it struck me this wasn't the most fitting topic to devote my last hour on earth to, so I began to think about you and your brother, and that's all I remember until I found my sheets were blue-green plastic."

"Ah darling. It *was* awful."

"Yes. Well. Anyhow. 'Have I woken on the bright morning of my disaster' isn't the thing to say. Or necessarily write about— Priam's roll-call of human catastrophe's taken care of that already. Which reminds me, you haven't said how that comic-*Agamemnon* of yours is getting on, what's this about Charles Ebury's helping you?"

" 'About' Charles, darling? how d'you mean?"

"How'd *he* happen to get in on it, what'd anybody mean!"

"But simply he very kindly offered to give advice if I needed it, heavens what else! He lectures on the *Oresteia* in his Greek Religions course as well as in his Greek Tragedy, darling he's a perfect adviser!"

"Well I read Greek too, what of it?—even Æschylus!"

"Oh but Pa you're busy—and anyway you're important! And also it was Amy knowing I was writing it sent Charles. Or practically. Why should I have bothered you, heavens!"

" 'Bother'?—good god, you're my daughter!"

"But darling all the more reason!"

"Well but what's this 'advice' you claim he's giving you dammit," the father complained.

"But heavens all sorts of suggestions! For instance Cassandra sings her first solo aria—woe woe behold her, King Priam's Bennington-educated daughter now a mere slave and concubine, and to this thug-witted provincial warlord, even in bed he talks geopolitics, *so* funny, and what Charles did was write some absolutely coleporterly extra lyrics for her, some of it he says lifted nearly word for word from Æschylus himself!"

Her father said politely, why, wonderful.

"Then Agamemnon is 'a morose and rumbling basso,' Charles says, and in his opening aria he complains ('in a grumpy and self-pitying roar,' Charles says it should be) about how middle-aged and put-upon he feels, what's he supposed to *do* with this damn' Cassandra!—of course being top trophy she *had* to be allotted to him as commander-in-chief, status is after all status, but why was it his luck to get *this* wincing little finishing-school intellectual! And look at this affair his wife has been having with his cousin in his absence—couldn't the silly bitch have picked somebody outside the royal succession to go to bed with? Why, all he had to do was fall down a stair and break his neck, and everybody'd think she'd murdered him to make the fellow king! The political fatuity he has to put up with! And when all he wants after ten years of war's a little peace and quiet—and a concubine who isn't so everlastingly avant-garde in bed!"

He said this hers or Ebury's?

"Mostly mine."

By god it was wonderful!—could be practically a satyr-play for the original *Oresteia!*

"That's what Charles says too, how did you know? And then we've thought up what's a *really* lovely twist—"

"Look, my sweet child, how do you collaborate or whatever, you and Ebury?"

"How?—but how do you mean, 'how'?"

"What could I mean dammit!—he come to your place, for instance? Or you to his!"

So naturally she opened her eyes at him. "But darling *Pa!*" she cried. "What could 'where' have to do with it! Except it's *my* typewriter I'm used to. But half the time neither of us goes anywhere, we just telephone, goodness. Oh Daddy am I tiring you?"

He mumbled *god* no.

"Then about the twist at the end? Because Orestes, see, comes home from graduate-school in Phocis, and he's just as much a young intellectual as Cassandra, so in Act Two they fall in love and sing a Liebesduett about the stuffiness of their parents. And in Act Three they elope back to the Troad—so of course then Agamemnon, in a great bellowing finale, has to muster the Greek host all over again, this time to get *his* girl back, oh it's lovely! Oh but Daddy I *am* tiring you!"

'Tiring' him? she never tired him! Dear god it was she and Botticelli epiphanies like her that kept him interested in staying alive, in this tedious place *and* out of it. No but by god *really* what a witty scenario—she was wonderful! And might he offer a suggestion too? for a possible curtain-effect? couldn't have Ebury making all the contributions, Classics prof or not! So what would she say to this, for the curtain coming down: as Agamemnon plunges off bellowing côté cour, why not have Clytemnestra and Ægisthus saunter off giggling côté jardin, hand in hand?

"Oh Daddy how perfect, Charles'll—"

"Well dammit Clytemnestra was after all Helen of Troy's sister, doesn't she deserve a little self-expression too?—aux jolis minois les baisers!"

"Oh Charles will love it!—he admires you terribly anyway you know. He says he particularly falls in love with your heroines, did I tell you?"

"Well don't let him fall in love with *you!*" he cried.

"*Pa!*" she reproved him, in sheer scandal.

So he mumbled something. Contrite, presumably.

"But darling I thought you liked him!"

. . . Nothing against the fellow. Nothing at all! Simply hadn't perhaps seen all that much of him. For an opinion. Except of course his being a wit. Which he was.

"And in the way *you* are, Daddy, haven't you noticed? Even his subconscious behaves like yours, goodness!—he told me he woke up the other day with it giving him the complete opening sentence for a story he wouldn't even consider writing either!"

What was a father to say.

"And he's just done this hilarious article on modern poetry which is exactly Daddy how you feel about it yourself, I mean he says there's so little tradition of craftsmanship that most of the poor gabbling practitioners don't even know they aren't even far enough along in their apprenticeships to realize tradition exists!"

He said by god *no!*

"And Charles is just as sarcastic about them as you are. Only he says he'll have to publish it under a nom de guerre, because of for instance Alec. Well, and of me. But how arrange it, so I said but I'll simply take it to Laura! Because don't you think? Oh and he has such a brilliant title for it, 'Mr. Molehill's Reasons For Writing,' isn't it lovely?"

. . . Why couldn't the fellow take it to Laura himself!

"But darling *no* reason, heavens! Except why shouldn't I do it for him? knowing her so much better! Being *family!*"

He said well but dear god *Alec* was a modern poet!

"Goodness, I'm being *unfaithful* you mean?" she laughed. "And with my very best friend's live-in—oh *Pa!*"

—But here the nurse swept efficiently in, looking dismissive and put-upon; so for that morning that was that.

5

Mrs. Tench-Fenton rang up her stepson next day at his faculty office, though this she seldom did, "because is this wretched hospital being *guarded* do you think, Alec, about poor Scrope's actual condition, what it truly is? he of course *is* getting I assume better isn't he? and Sibylla they must have told something definite by now surely!" interrupting one of his term-paper consultations ("Non-U and Demotic in Philip Larkin"), and this was a student who, besides an enchanting bosom, had an entrancing lisp. "One gets nothing *nothing* from doctors, he could be even *dying* and you couldn't tell whether they did or didn't know whether they as much as knew!"

He said, well—

"But can't your sweet Sibylla insist a little more? because how am *I* to! You are I mean so lucky to have her, that darling, but mightn't you perhaps suggest to her— Well, the man *is* your own father-in-law, Alec!"

He said but—

"Isn't *she* worried poor sweet he may for instance not even think seriously enough about himself (and you *know* how he can *not!*) to tell us what they may have told *him?* and when I am half frantic!"

He said—

"Alec he never had even a chest pain till this!—and I've known him from *years*, even, before I'd as much as met your infuriating great angel of a father! Or said I'd marry him— *imagine* not telling me you existed, when there you were all the time, off at that hair-raising permissive prep-school, really how do Quakers justify the means of whatever their ends are! No but Alec is he— Oh *how* is he? and can't you do anything but mumble? Or is there some student with you."

He smiled at the girl (who smiled obediently back).

"Because *I* never know whether you're off in one of your inarticulate brooding intervals or not, goodness your lovely speech-less father babbled, compared! But Alec *besides* being sick with worry poor darling like all of us about Scrope is Sibylla can you tell me seeing to the housekeeping side of things at his flat mean-time?—I mean the poor man's laundry to be picked up from wherever and for instance how much is there rotting in his ice-box. Oh and has she any idea whether he may have let that Yale young woman have a key?"

He appeared to search his memory.

"Because you know how he is! Or hasn't Sibylla are you try-ing to tell me even asked him whether! Is the silly child— Oh Alec you *can't* mean she knows so little about her father that she thinks he's having something like an affair with the girl, so she's diffident about asking!"

He said he—

"And when she told me the girl seems even considerate about not disturbing him? heavens! Monday mornings she's up dark-of-the-dawn as far as she can make out, and makes herself breakfast and lays out everything for *his*, with a little thank-you note (sometimes in Danish—'playfully,' Scrope supposes), and is off to Grand Central before he'd even consider opening his eyes. And writes up her weekend notes on the train back to New Haven. Of course what *sort* of notes about a man like Scrope this girl can possibly be taking, well *yes* Alec who wouldn't wonder! —it could hardly be just routine time-motion average-minutes between the beset man's breakfast and the day's first word-on-paper mutterings, but who ever knows with these people? even sociologists haven't studied what sociologists study have they? But Alec an *affair* with her? hoh!"

He said um.

"Oh with any normally light-minded flighty young woman well yes Alec naturally of course—'unripeness is all.' But an affair with a creature who for all he knows is carrying out his humane statistics to three sigmas—what *can* Sibylla be thinking of!"

Her stepson sighed, eyes on his student (whose eyes were cast down).

"And in particular since we all Alec know what's certain is, he's taking his wretched wordless mental notes on *her*, oh he can be outrageous! One never knows *when* some innocent offhand remark one's made to him in perfect decency won't turn up in his dialogue in a, well, in a different context altogether, and the shock when you remember the situation *and* sometimes the state you were in when you actually said it, and realize what he's— Because think of all the ones you may *not* be sure it wasn't you who said, and people *reading* them, oh he's detestable!"

He of course, as was civil, was silent.

"And how am I not to worry for him for *sensible* reasons, poor old angel! For one thing, and even if it sounds superstitious,

Sibylla says he's taken to being so, well, being *rude* of all things about God, when he's never bothered his head about religion five minutes in his whole life—because Sibylla says *why* suddenly, is he worried about himself seriously? Because there *is* his age. He's been composing sardonic little couplets, she says, for instance

> God (Zeus, Iddio, Bog, Dieu, Gott)
> Does as He pleases. We may not

which he actually seems to *resent*, she says. She'd no idea he even thought enough about God to be down on Him. He said that bloody-minded old Jewish smiter was bad enough, but were St. Paul's book-length regulations much of an improvement?—so childish really, Alec, imagine! Of course Sibylla says he was amusing too: Creation he admitted was an attractive idea in its way, everything fresh and new, and archangels fluttering in and out with ecological and demographic suggestions of one sort and another. But then he said, that was back *then*; and what we seem to have got is this bureaucracy of angels distributing computerized damnations. So my dear what is one to think?"

And so on, until presently the student mumbled something apologetic and bashful (as to a poet) and left.

6

One midmorning, after a class, Sibylla Urquhart rang up Charles Ebury and said had he a minute? because, first, her father had a beautiful curtain for the libretto she wanted to tell him, and second, to read him something—"because remember you said what you call the 'dream girls' in Daddy's novels are actually symbols? which help him recall and reconstruct the feelings he felt, not the particular perhaps girls."

"*I* made this meta-critical remark?"

"Yes Charles you did, and so then you said if I was worried about this Yale involvement of his, though you said *you* weren't in the least, why didn't I read up on the traits of the heroines in his novels? and if they didn't match hers, stop worrying; but what it's *done* somehow is make me think I don't perhaps know anything really about him at all! Oh and when here the old darling is, so *ill*, Charles!"

He instantly said should he come round.

"Oh I didn't mean to make you *concerned*, goodness!" she cried, in a happy voice. "When it's oh probably you know nothing but delayed shock don't you suppose?—like remember I told you the time I found out Daddy'd had this devastating-them-both affair with Alec's sweetie of a mother."

He put in '—stepmother.'

"How can one *not* be involved in one's parents' amours!— even didn't I tell you I was a tiny *child* when I heard Mummy laughing with a friend of hers about 'the *tedium* of all those frantic little bitches in heat over my husband,' what age was I?— anyway I remember I had to look 'tedium' up in the dictionary, I thought was it for instance a new dirty word, what could I have been, seven? eight?"

He snorted, amused.

"Oh *well*," she conceded. "No but anyway Charles I've done what you said why not try, researched their dreamy traits, his girls', and I came on this very early one, early I mean if she was real, so it's this passage about her I wanted to read to you and see what you think. Or am I interrupting you in something, what were you doing?"

"Wondering whether to interrupt you."

"Goodness, how kind, and you even sound as if you were, such nice manners, Charles!"

He was silent.

"But what!" she said, surprised.

"Not 'manners,' " he said, lightly. "Never mind. What early girl?"

"In that wartime-London novel of Daddy's, and the hero's uncle had given him a letter of introduction to her m'ma. So he sends it round and then calls—

and there, in the practiced blandishment of her cool young white and gold, was Lady Sophia.

Daddy *loves* that word 'blandishment'!

How tiresome of M'ma to be late and not there! And when how kind of him to have called! His old connoisseur of an uncle had by god told the truth—an elegant dish she was, poised and uninnocent, wanton blue-eyed gaze and all.

Of course the old uncle had had an affair with the mother years before; typical Pa! Well, the girl's married to

a splendid young brute named Hamish FitzEdmund, a rowing-hearty type with the usual brigade-of-guards manner, but he was a subaltern at HQ Cairo, and she was holding her beauty's court in her m'ma's drawing room or levee in her own. Two dozen other young officers were in various stages of fuming rut or suicidal despair over her—

Does she sound like any of Daddy's usual girls to you either? And then listen to this:

She was trained to please, as for centuries only her class has been trained to please. But she had too many generations of libertine ladyships behind her to fancy taking a lover anything but ordinary good breeding: what was one trained *for*?

I mean do you believe in her? Isn't she just sort of novel-character real?—not 'alive,' just with the type-traits you expect from the type."

"You believe in the stylization," he said.

". . . I do?"

"You make the required adjustments and assumptions. The way you assume the non-existent fourth wall in a stage-set. Look, stylizing's been here from the beginning, Æschylus and all—if you don't see his Cassandra's a total stylization, think if Stendhal or good god Flaubert had written her! What do you think even our Cassandra is!"

Sibylla was silent.

And for so long that he said, "You still there?"

"Oh *yes*. Just I hoped you were going on."

"About Cassandra?"

"Or anything. I like to hear you talk."

So he was silent. Until presently he said, "Well, but about understanding your father?"

"Oh. Yes, well. Except I suppose this Lady Sophia wasn't all that explaining-him, was it. I just thought I'd read it to you, is all. And see what you thought. Well I *happened* on it! And you did suggest I 'research.' So I just felt I'd like to read it to you. Is all," she finished.

Then they were both silent.

And for so long it as good as became a stylization.

But at last, "Ah look," he said, "this is God *knows* à l'improviste, but will you have lunch with me?"

". . . 'lunch'?"

"If only to— Since we can't I suppose do anything much more *than* that about whatever-it-is, can we."

". . . Oh Charles."

"Well but can we?"

". . . No I suppose really not."

"But at least at lunch we— Because what you rang me up about wasn't really *what* you rang me up about, was it."

She was silent.

"So come to at least lunch?"

She still said nothing.

"Squarcialuppi's? Les Piérides? Five-Four-Three?"

"Oh Charles I *can't*, I'm seeing *Daddy!*"

"Well then tomorrow?"

"Oh pet you don't understand—I *take* Daddy lunch, the hospital kitchen puts him into rages. So I make him his particular daubes and navarins and heat them in the nurses' pantry. And today it's a coq au vin."

". . . I see."

"And I stay with him while he eats, oh Charles forgive me? Because I'm afraid I am sort of caught! Or at least until Daddy's nearer out and home again."

"But then?"

"Well but those first days home—"

"But good *god*, Sibylla," he cried at her, "am I to assume that if you and I were across a table at Les Piérides instead of at the ends of a damn' telephone cable all we'd do is gaze at each other sadly?—what *is* this!"

But this outburst she of course at once countered with the proprieties. "But what's *what*, goodness!—and so ominous-sounding, Charles!"

" 'Ominous'!"

"Well but what am I to think? When have I ever 'gazed sadly' at you!"

"You abashing me?" he said, and laughed.

"Well *anybody* listening to you!" she rebuked him, smiling.

So he said ah well but to go back then, what was this new finale her ingenious father had suggested for the libretto; so she described it for him, and presently they rang off.

7

That same morning, though after a different class, Alec Urquhart rang up Amy Hallam and said (so dispiritedly she hardly heard him) was she busy? or could he come see her about something, and she said all she was doing was shorten a skirt, would he mind a sewing-machine in a flustered bedroom? she *loved* seeing him, even about something; but when presently he arrived he looked so altogether cast down she was too surprised to kiss him.

"But Alec sweetie this *gloom?*" she protested. "But what possible— Oh sit on the bed where I can *see* you, goodness!" she told him, for he was looming there over her, gazing down it seemed wordless with woe. "No but what *is* this?" she demanded, concerned, as he sat. "Heavens something *that* desponding?— and when Alec you're looking so huge and handsome I could fall swooning into your arms with helpless love!"

He gaped at her, stunned.

She was astonished. "But Alec *sweetie!*" she cried. "What *can* it be!" (For indeed he appeared overwhelmed.) "What I said?

—except goodness, said what? I mean heavens-said-what! That I could swoon at you?—oh dear don't tell me you're *upset* I might!"

He mumbled something—hopeless, it sounded.

"But I *wouldn't*, who'd even think I would? even the time Sibylla spotted that lovely crush I had on you she didn't! Oh Alec don't tell me she still thinks I— Oh *not* that it's something *worse*, oh *no!*"

What could he have said but what could he say! He was mute.

". . . but with *me?*" this best friend babbled. "When how possibly! And when simply we *haven't*, Alec! And when is this to have happened, even! And how—am I supposed to have seduced you? and when I don't even dream about you any more, oh *darling* Alec how appalling!"

Though what could he say.

"Oh poor sweetie can't you do anything but sit there gulping? —so *sad*, and when it was such an innocent crush! Like *everybody's*, and I never do anything about them anyway, oh why have I the fidelity of the raven! And it wasn't an adulterous crush *ever*, just I used to carry your latest published poem around with me in my handbag. For company. And to wordlessly tell it I wordlessly adored you. All the time of course feeling awful at *not* feeling awful about Sibylla. But then I sort of knew I didn't feel genuinely awful because probably I wasn't ever actually going to sleep with you, I hope you don't mind, it wasn't you-as-such I wasn't going to sleep with, goodness every time I saw you I was faint with longing, but just I didn't seem to feel convinced it was likely I'd hand myself over to myself like that. So then I felt better about wordlessly adoring you. And then, well, in bed with Charles I realized I always forgot about you entirely, I hope you won't mind that either, so anyhow being *that* heartless I felt better. Except I still felt like a dopey teenager. Until I got over you. Except I've never I guess got *that* over, maybe I never will, I'll always remember with sweet sadness my crush on you. Because who says nostalgia doesn't change the part of you that's being nostalgic, I think about how I *thought* about going to bed with you, and could I be any more tender than that even if we had? I mean it's how I felt not whether I did what I felt. *Am* I supposed to have seduced you? Or is it you me? Oh dear. Oh *dear!* Do you ever seduce your students?—like Charles, if he does?"

He muttered something unintelligible.

"Or is it they I suppose seduce you. Or I mean try to. *There!*" she said to the machine, lining the seam up again. "Or do you just avoid the situation—so *wicked* and cruel of you Alec, when the poor girl's decided on you! *I* thought I adored you didn't I?— and adored *you*, not your poetry, goodness I don't think I always really *read* the poem of yours I was faithfully carrying around, I just blissfully felt I knew you by heart, you *see* how dopey? Oh well, Charles says since Joyce even freshman girls have epiphanies. Oh Alec how *can* they imagine we are lovers! Charles is my true sweetie, how could he suspect me? Or Sibylla you? What *are* we to do, to be innocent?—how can either of us make love *like* a faithful spouse without the performing's affecting the performance!"

He had no answer—the question having, in any case, merely stated a dilemma.

8

One afternoon, later that week, a delicious child named Amanda Hallam (but called Mimi) and a gangling boy named Richard Scrope Townshend III rolled stickily apart in a bedroom they had borrowed in Blair Hall, and he said ". . . *whoooh!*" and gaped at the ceiling vacant-eyed, for he in particular of this pair of Princeton freshmen had still, for this sort of thing, some polish to acquire.

So they lay there—she too, for the moment—dozing.

But in time she stretched, arching her slim back in a murmur of luxury, wriggling her toes. She opened her eyes, and, swallowing a yawn, appeared to think.

So presently she lolled her head on the pillow toward the stuporous boy.

Whose jaw hung ajar, slack. He might have been about to snore. She was amused.

And so, finally, rolled up onto an elbow and contemplated him with lazy indulgence, eyes assessing his young-male length detail by detail. She could have been appraising a work in progress. And perhaps signing it, for she put out a ladylike fingertip, and, on his belly, lightly traced an M.

His flesh winced.

She said, "*My* you sweat!" and wiped her finger in his hair.

His eyes came open, glazed.

"You're practically *trickling!*" she giggled. "And look at me, you great slop—you were trickling onto *me!*"

He stared, still lost.

"Oh and you're trickling *yet!*" she taunted happily—and with practiced ease slid up and knelt astride his moist middle, toes tucked in along his flanks as elegantly as a jockey's.

He yelped *Hey!* and came to.

"So *sad* you're so messy!"

He reared his head and stared down his length to her, sheepish, saying, ". . . am?"

"*And* so bony!" she told him, shifting in the saddle.

He mumbled, ". . . aw, Mimi," as in appeasement.

So she smiled down at him, poised there; and for a long moment they were silent again, smiling faintly, both—a girl riding a dolphin they could have been, a marble from Methymna, brought for some Roman fountain lost in time, and, for that later taste, Arion a girl.

"So then anyway you can just stop freaking at me about Amy!" she decreed, and for obedience.

He made an indeterminate swallowing sound.

"Because I certainly *can too* bug her bedroom if I want to, goodness she's my sister! And it isn't as if I'm going to *tell* anybody what I hear!"

He said, meekly, "Well but you told me."

"Not what was on the actual tape I didn't! So it's not what

she *said*. And naturally it won't be about *her* in my term-paper, stupid—we *generalize* people in Sociology!"

He appeared to reflect on this. But he said, "Yuh but *bug* your own sister's apartment?—that's *real* flakey!"

"Not her apartment, her bed!"

"Well, jesus, her bed—just for some crappy term-paper? *Jesus*, Mimi, where were you brought up!"

"All right then tell me how *else* I can get to actually compare generational affective vocabularies!—you can't *ask!* I have to compare all the subjective-erotic topic-ratios too—so *how* else!"

"Compare with what."

"Well, with our generation. Naturally. But also I thought why not with D. H. Lawrence, I'm tired of Proust. Anyway he was *old-fashioned* gay, so that would screw up my glossary of demotic input too."

"What's 'demotic'?"

"Four letters."

He pondered. "Ah but anyway *look*," he said finally, "it's poor. It's just *poor!*"

"It is *not!* How *do* generations differ? Professor Staling said it will be a fascinating special demonstration!"

"Another durdy old man!"

"Oh, well, professors. But so what. Just they've all read *Lolita* and they think *that's* it. Amy says when she was a freshman she had a professor who couldn't seem to tell her from that sort of White Russian daydream either."

"From *what?*"

"Well he *was* a White Russian. Vladimir something—he wanted her to call him Vovo. He'd say, 'You 'ave never wish to making laaahv with Russian man?'—so wistful, she said. She felt sorry for him, sort of. Only of course not *that* sorry. Oh Richard your mouth *is* so pretty!" she exulted, and traced the line of it with a fingertip. "No but then Amy really baffles me sex-wise. Because Richard on that very first tape I played back, there she was, not *in* bed but in her bedroom, which she's always *neurotic* about men in except Charles, and Richard it was your uncle!"

He said, blank, "Christ what uncle!"

"How many uncles have you got?—Alec, silly!"

"Hey, Alec's not my uncle!"

"Your aunt's husband's not your uncle?"

"Sibylla's not my aunt, she's my father's half-sister. So what's her husband?—he's not anything!"

"He would be in New Guinea, among the Arrhoa! And among the Neshaminy he'd be your wan'h-toc."

"Where'd you get all this—that same crappy course?"

"Listen, do you want to hear about them in Amy's bedroom or don't you?"

"Well he's *not my uncle!*"

"Well and he hasn't *done* anything yet either, but they're certainly going to!"

"Yeah? how can you tell?"

"I can tell—verbally she was all *over* him!"

"Nuts, you can't tell!"

"I can too! I'm not some dumb *boy!* Listen, she was pretending to sew a skirt or something, so she had her sewing-machine between them, unconsciously she goes in for symbols all the time anyway, so it was there as a barrier, to help drive him wild, goodness a sewing-machine in a bedroom? why else! And *then* Richard all she talked about was this swooning crush she'd had on him, but eventually she'd got over it, except she was afraid she hadn't got over it *really*. And oh, nostalgia and stuff, oh Richard it was

lurid, really she was disgusting, I mean what a fuss that generation turns out to make about it!"

He said unh.

"But when she has *Charles?* oh she's out of her *head* sexually!
—she moons over a towering hunk like your uncle when *any*
woman would want lovely Charles, I don't care if Alec *is* a very
getting-famous poet."

Well he was no clod.

"No but if Amy's going to have this do with him, what about
Charles?—maybe *I'll* have to keep him in the family, hoh!"

Her young man was scandalized. "Screw some guy three
times your age?—*jesus*, Mimi!"

"Oh taaaah, what about that friend of your mother's on the
Cape last summer!—are you so dumb you haven't even worked
out yet how you got seduced?"

So he mumbled something.

"Anyway she did a good job on you, what are you grumping
about?—d'you think I'd be in bed with a *freshman* if she hadn't?
So shut up! You didn't even know what was happening to you.
Oh you're all so dumb and helpless! Oh well of course since *then*
you've got lovely," she conceded, and squeezed him with her
knees. "No but about Charles I don't *feel* I feel cynical, it's just
that maybe I owe it to myself to fall in *love*, to see. I mean Charles
has this epigram, 'It's disillusion that turns girls into women,' so I
keep thinking at what point, sort of, is this going to happen to *me*.
What are you looking like that for?"

He said well jesus, keep him tuned!

"Oh come aaaahn!" she said. "Would even Charles be forever
either?—what's so awesome! Anyway listen, what time did you
tell those two wisps we'd give them their room back? Because
how about making you a believer again?"

So, as a child of the technological age, he looked at his wristwatch.

"Or aren't you up to it!"

But to this he replied as idiomatically as if an English major already, and the intellectual segment of the afternoon concluded.

Except that, in due course dressing again, suddenly she shrieked, "Oh god I forgot to take out my *lenses!* . . ." so they issued forth at last, beneath the spalling majesty of Witherspoon, snickering their heads off.

9

Mrs. Tench-Fenton rang up Charles Ebury from one of her corporation's Sabre-Liners and breathed a caressing "Oh Charles . . ." because she *could* call him Charles couldn't she? she'd not thought of him as anything else since that night he'd entranced her about Ovid at Sibylla's party for Miss Hallam's editor's upsetting divorce, the things young women *did*, and anyhow her darling Sibylla had talked so practically glowingly about him when she brought her his brilliant piece on modern poetry (and which *couldn't* be funnier!) that she almost felt she almost knew him well, *not* just as a party talk-to, it was devastatingly funny, he'd had her laughing since take-off in St. Louis and here they were halfway to Santa Fe (not that opera was one of her weaknesses, it always seemed to be so badly written, but culturally one was helpless, and the *town* was charming) because from the wit of his title *on* it was magisterial, 'Mr. Molehill's Reasons For Writing' was goodness so *true!* and then this he'd said about Samuel Beckett, this now where was it, of course Beckett wasn't technically a poet, oh where *was* it? but his sort of drama— Oh here it was!

Beckett has only to intone 'Nowhere is now here,' and the professors of Comparative Profundity are off—the transit of the letter W from the brow of one semantic unit to the sad butt of the other has become a statement of God's plan.

—oh she adored it, and then the way on this next page he *demolished* academic criticism—

in the gesturing and excited hands of insight-mongers and meta-readers and sub-Hegelians and moonlighting sociologists and even a stray shrink, in a pandemonium of happiest self-display

—oh *Charles*, but for alas *her* readership? goodness he didn't imagine readers read did he! quite aside from the delicate circumstance (or was it a quandary!) that her own dear stepson was so splendidly a modern poet himself poor boy, so in practice had Sibylla perhaps not thought before bringing her such a dilemma-making piece, she herself had even for a moment said to herself how Sibylla must admire *him*, had he enchanted her too?—though why hadn't he simply brought her the manuscript himself, was he *shy?* No but in any case, what she thought he'd promised he'd do for her, at the party, was fifteen hundred words about *Ovid*'s poems, the ones about making love, he'd made him sound as if all she or any woman would ever want to do was gratefully lose her heart to the man, ancient Roman or not!

Well, he said, apparently Ovid—

"Because you told me in particular that he was a man who simply, well, who *liked* women not just loved us, remember? or was I just meant to understand," she laughed, "that you were telling me you did too?"

He said well Ovid said—

But "Oh Charles," she teased him, "men who actually do like women you *know* are terribly bad for us, you're so few and far between you're disorienting, I mean are we really to *believe* you think we're people or something?—so we begin to mistrust our very ability to read signals, it's *unsettling!* heavens can we have been wrong all along somehow about men?—because our total relationship *automatically* we've thought what's it been but fending off such endless low marauders! So then how on earth are we to—is the word 'comport' ourselves? I haven't heard it in so long do I even remember how to use it correctly! anyway I mean we think, Look, if he's not attacking me what am I defending myself for, heavens! So in a sort of happy daze we stop defending. And then of course see what happens. But oh Charles you *know* this, you're not like those fumbling Howells-ish characters in Henry James who have to have minor characters explain things to them all the time, you're— Oh *damn!*" she yelped, "my pilot says the ground's saying— Oh Charles it's the call I've had in for San Francisco, it's ready, oh *damn* when we were having this lovely talk but I *must* go, there are four *legal*-pad sheets of details to settle with them before lunch, but you *will* do me your lovely love-making Ovid, promise *promise* you will?"

He said he—

"And oh when also I so wanted to ask *you* about how Scrope is really, almost Charles I'm afraid to leave town, not knowing, but I thought—well you and Sibylla are seeing so much of each other if nothing else, over I mean this libretto of hers of course, that doesn't she ever say *what* the doctors think? I know he's in a room now like anybody, not cardiac care, but he's still being monitored, and surely they'd detach the poor darling if they— Oh the ground's *shouting* for me, oh Charles *sweetie* goodby, *do me your Ovid!*" she wailed, and vanished.

10

When Amy Hallam came to see Scrope in his still sternly monitored room she brought him a gardenia, and went so far as to kiss his cheek in greeting.

So he dutifully grumbled, why, what a sweet she was, every time he saw her he found himself regretting he wasn't a couple of hundred years younger again.

But she said, "But goodness what *was* that I passed going out coming in!"

His ghostly solacer?—the Rev. Ms. somebody. Or was the word 'solacess'? Ah, well, pretty enough girl he supposed. Just been ordained, if that mattered.

"But Scrope sweetie, *wide-eyed* from you?"

Oh, that. Theological petulance, who in God's name knew? —what'd the blasted girl come bothering him for!—he dying or something? Anyway all he'd done was ask her was she tempting him to salvation, looking the way she did, or was the devil tempting him in the other direction by making her so tempting?

"Oh Scrope you *said* that?"

Why not?—normal masculine homage, surely? First duty of

man, *he*'d been brought up believing, was to assure any girl God had made as delectable as that, that she *was* as delectable as that. Could even quote himself to that effect: 'Women should be told regularly, like bells,' to parody Noel Coward. Or didn't homage from a man his age count as homage. No, but this girl—once she'd got over whatever sub-Pauline pet it was she was in, she'd look in her glass wouldn't she? Which might even start a musing doubt whether God's work *was* what God had in mind when creating her!

As however none of this had much to do with either of Miss Hallam's reasons for visiting the man, she at once began a soothing transition to what were.

Having, besides, found him in *this* sort of mood!

"Oh but Scrope *sweetie*," she cooed, "but when I was so hoping you'd help me with something?—and here you are all patronizing and cross!"

'Patronizing'!

"Well, to *her*, weren't you? And well you do sometimes like to sound as if your programs for women were more sensible than our own, even about making love, as it usually seems to be, though of course why not, but I have something I hope you'll be a sweetie and discuss, because I'm stuck in a story I've been thinking about, about age 'differences.' "

Discuss? Glad to! Whose age differences?

"Well actually anybody's, of different sexes, for instance how do you see younger women and girls as being?"

. . . As being what?

"As just *being*. Their ambience, sort of. Being the younger *way* they are. As less maybe how you're used to."

He was amused: dear god, hadn't he, a month ago, told her he hadn't the ghost of an idea about that generation? Ask his

Gael of a son-in-law, why didn't she. Or Charles—they both taught the creatures!

"But they wouldn't themselves be at that age difference. And anyhow this particular story— Oh for instance suppose that girl minister wasn't a *minister*, and she suddenly adored you and you had an affair, different ages and all, would you feel about her the *way* you would if she were fifteen or twenty years older? Or say twenty-five," she added, in generosity.

What was she doing, interviewing him?

"But Scrope think of the way you write about them, I remember the very phrase the first time I noticed how often you do use it—in this novel your hero's in his pantry getting more ice for a party and this girl's followed him, she's infatuated with him though he doesn't know it yet, and here's how you introduced her, it's lovely—'the door had swung open and swung gently to again, and in had stepped this beautiful child'—*so* skillful, but 'child'? she's in Radcliffe! So is this just technique or *do* you think of them that way?"

. . . well, a certain docileness had to be conveyed, he supposed, yes. Demureness perhaps too? Still, in that sort of relationship, a kind of daughterly deference he'd assume was at work. Of course the corollary was ludicrous—imagine a love affair in which you found yourself muttering, 'Dammit this *can't* be the best thing for the child!' as you clambered into bed!

"But do they feel this older man knows more?—so he's complacent at teaching things as well as at being adored?"

So he snorted—dear god what sort of thing went on in her stories! For all he knew, anyway, girls who fell in love with older men were a special category as much as for instance just working their way through a phase. For dammit look: were they more 'mature'—so that they went for you as being worldlier? Or were they, instead, so much less mature that they went for you as being Daddy! He hoped (might he say?) she wasn't consulting him about some such state of her own! Or was she.

"Oh sweetie when I *love* men? No but *what* ages do you think of as being this girls/young-women category? And *treat* that way, the way the hero in your novel treats what's-her-name, sort of like a valuable pet, I mean he couldn't be more considerate or nicer to her, but doesn't he think she's up to him emotionally or something? Why *doesn't* he make love with her! The woman he's in love with is *just* as silly, only she's forty, oh *do* you see what I'm trying to find out?"

Dammit, he wasn't his characters!

"But you must have some age at which *you* think of us as knowing 'what's good for us' as well as you think *you* do—and consequently stop patronizing us? I mean Scrope men love women but what is the *difference* in how somebody like you sees himself as loving differently at different ages? Or do you just subjectively and arbitrarily decide on sight who's a femme sérieuse for you and who isn't?"

Well, he said, the—

"Am I one?"

He said, smiling at her, had he ever had the misplaced effrontery to try to find out? But 'patronize' implied a value-judgment he never made. Simply he felt women should be thought of as ballerinas; they then responded with every grace. What more they were, *than* that, one discovered as they decided one deserved. Care for an epigram?—she could have that one.

So she looked at him. And seemed to brood.

And finally, "Oh well," she said, and smiled at him. "Anyway I'm *so* glad you're so much better."

At least no worse.

"You're wonderful, to be consulted. And discuss."

Pleasure to!

"Oh but I hope it hasn't tired you?"

He said what nonsense.

She seemed about to go.

But then, "But there is though *one* other thing," she came out with, instead. "Not to consult about, exactly, just it's something you might think of some way to help with if I tell you. Because Scrope partly it's about Sibylla, only it simply isn't something I can think of any way to talk to her about, I mean this is *unbelievable!*"

But good god, he said, in some alarm, she mean something *wrong?*—Sibylla not having a serious spat with Alec or that sort of thing he hoped was she?

She gaped at him, lost.

" 'A spat'!" she marveled. "Oh but Scrope oh *dear* what—"

For God's sake not *leaving* the fellow she didn't mean did she! —even *for* some lout she'd taken a fancy to?

"Oh but *Scrope!*" she wailed, "it's Sibylla thinks *I'm* having an affair! With *Alec!*"

So, parentally or not, the man was taken aback.

"And probably my darling Charles thinks so too!"

He mumbled well God *bless!* As called for.

"But how do you mean?" she begged him. "Because how *can* they think such a thing! Alec and I don't even dream about each other! And the awful part is, what can we merely *do?*—plant ourselves beaming before them saying sweeties we have something wonderful to tell you out of the blue?—we're *un*-having an affair?"

That he certainly saw!

"Especially since one of the reasons we're sure they do think we are is that they've been so unbelievably careful not to give the slightest sign they do!"

He said um.

"And of course your dearest friend's husband *is* your very likeliest lover of anybody, you *see* him so constantly, and his things lying around keep making you think of him undressing. And of in bed with her. And then, well, it happens I—oh dear I wouldn't tell this to anybody but you but I even did have this wild crush on Alec once."

Did, huh; well!

"I adored him for *weeks!* Only Scrope I had I guess *such* a crush I was too terrified of him to think about normally seducing him or anything, can you imagine such a state!"

He said well God bless indeed! But hadn't Sibylla suspected this, uh, this unholy passion at the time?

"Oh no."

Then how'd she happen to now?

"Well *Alec* thinks, from something he thinks she let slip without meaning to— Oh I *can't* tell you!"

So then, for now she seemed not far from helpless tears, for a moment they were silent.

Finally he said well it *was* dreadful for her.

"And I did, once, tell Charles a dream I had about Alec. So, working on Sibylla's libretto together the way they are, Charles could have told her."

So once again there seemed to be little to say.

Though ah, well, he said presently, he supposed one ought to entertain a decent concern for one's offsprings' marriages and the like. Men and women had no pleasure in life like each other;

nobody but hysterical crackpots like St. Paul ever suggested anything else. But had fidelity all that to do with it? Look, if all that
our piety-simple writs and prescripts about adultery produced was
a divorce rate ten times the civilized average abroad, perhaps we
should explore the hypothesis that it was an unsung blessing!
Binas habeatis amicas, said Ovid—have two loves, and you're a
slave to neither. Well, but he himself meant turn Ovid round—
with two loves you grow *tired* of neither, and, as things go between men and women, you therefore stay married. And the
social structure preserves its stable decencies. So, as a natural
bonus—

"Is this your *Vanity Fair* piece?"

He said yes. So as a cultural bonus, the *family* is preserved.
What a pity Mrs. Tench-Fenton didn't take the piece—among
other nice bits it had an elderly-rake-sounding final paragraph he
was particularly pleased with—

"I don't perhaps get the reports from the field I used to," a
graying classmate said to me not long ago, "but by god I see
no signs of my kind of woman's becoming an endangered
species!"

Ah, well, anyway, he did hope Sibylla wasn't going to be, well,
for example upset? Had she back then, when she'd had this
ungovernable passion for Alec before?

"Oh no."

Well, it baffled him.

And he wished he could cheer her up; she was a sweet.
Would it he wondered amuse her to hear a rejection his agent
had just sent him from a French publisher? There'd been a
proposal for a translation of his next to last.

On y prend un plaisir réel, à condition de comprendre un argot pratiqué entre l'Hôtel Pierre et Washington Square: du Giraudoux de Manhattan.

Giraudoux?—he *that* much of an archaism abroad too? . . . And what was that 'argot'? *His* dialogue 'argot'? He'd wondered what they'd make of the language his subconscious sometimes came up with!—that very morning, for instance, an opening sentence as cockeyed as it was typical!

My old man was made a living for by a Little Rock call-girl named Prairie Anthum, but it was the garbage route put me through Yale.

She edified? Yes. Well. No but then what was book for jealousy in her generation? If for example Sibylla turned out not to be jealous, would that be because she was a liberated young woman and above any such degrading tradition? Dear god, she could just as easily be tired of Alec! . . .

And so on.

Till finally Miss Hallam began to smile, wanly anyway, and he said well at least *somehow* he seemed to have cheered her up! so shortly she kissed him almost fondly, and left.

11

That weekend, and this had been for purposes of research as much as for the hell of it (was there all that plus, sexwise, in spending the night together too?), Mimi Hallam and Richard Scrope Townshend III were house-sitting the Institute For Advanced Study pied-à-terre of her math instructor, who commuted from Las Vegas. The apartment had disappointed them: in particular, for their specific research, there was no double bed; aside moreover from a bust of Diophantos in travertine the humane amenities were bleakly wanting, the fellow's field being 'assorted sequestrations' in the cyclic-decomposition theorem of modules. They had nevertheless, being responsible children, stayed on. As taught one did.

Also they had made do, trundling the twin beds together and flumping the mattresses side by side across.

So, now, on these, Mimi was sprawling on her elbows, chin in her hands, drowsily listening to her bedfellow (sprawled on his back beside her) explain in exasperated detail how his father *kept* bugging him!—last week snapping if he *had* to have an elementary something for an elective why in God's name not

Elementary Russian the way *he* had, what good was this goddam Elementary Mandarin to anybody! and then last night jesus he'd rung him up *again* about going to see his grandfather, poor old guy'd been put back in intensive care and was or *wasn't* he going to see him before he maybe died!—when for god sakes how was he to get away, with two midterms Monday! Anyhow what could you think up to talk about with anybody old?

She murmured, "*Mmm*," and yawned.

"And then the way my father makes me what he calls clean up my language, visiting Grampa, like for Sunday lunches in summer—it fucking wears me out!"

She said, idly, "So but anyway what happened," almost as if having listened.

"Well, see, he was supposed to be better. Only then there was this girl priest kept visiting him, and my father says Grampa was too polite to tell her to keep the hell out."

Miss Hallam blew a soft *fffffffth* at a white fluff of pillow-feather in the hollow of his shoulder.

"Hey!" he complained.

"Why do you always need dusting!"

"Aw, Mimi," he grumbled.

"So well what *happened* then."

"Well finally he gave up being polite and bellowed at her. So then he had chest pains."

"Goodness," she said lazily, and yawned again.

So he yawned too.

And said, "Yes, well, jesus—people *at* you," and was silent. "Though you can see the poor old guy's point, at that, I guess," he added, generously.

They were silent.

But presently he stretched, as in purest luxury, limb by long young limb, and smiled at her, a question. And as she gazed back at him in what seemed womanly forbearance, why should he not have shifted a near shoulder, and slid a humble hand, palm up, under her sleek belly, in adoration and entreaty?

But she was simply amused.

"No."

"Aw, Mimi."

"Intermission's not over."

"It's *over* over!"

"Then why doesn't it feel like it."

"Feels to *me!*"

"As if you counted!"

"Aw, *Mimi*," he mumbled, as in hopeless love.

"And don't argue!"

So he drew back his hand, in abasement, dashed.

"That's better," she said kindly, and kissed the tip of his nose. "No but about your grandfather, listen you'll never *guess* what the very first tape picked up about his heart attack. Amy told Charles your Aunt Sibylla—"

"She's *not* my aunt!"

"—said she'd figured out what it must have been caused it, oh and this is wild!"

"Well jesus he's just old anyway."

"No *not* just that, no there's for weeks been this girl from Yale, well she's really a professor, she's doing a *book* on your grandfather, you didn't know? anyway she comes down from New Haven every weekend to study him and just moves *in!* Amy says she leaves crumbs all over the kitchen counters. And eggshells in the sink-strainer. And the bedroom smells of she thinks it's *Opium*, anyway it seems she's been sleeping with your grandfather every weekend for *weeks!*—so Sibylla said obviously he, well, *you* know, he overdid."

Her bedfellow was shocked.

"You simple?" he cried. "Look, jesus, old men *can't!*" in tones of scandal.

"Well it obviously doesn't seem they always can't! Anyway what are you so outraged about? Amy said Sibylla said she'd dropped by your grandfather's one Sunday nearly noon and the place was a mess, and this girl (who she said is *very* sexy) looked practically swoony, she was getting their breakfast in a dream, she looked as if they'd—"

"I don't care—old men can't!"

"How do *you* know!"

"Everybody knows!"

"Taaaah, how can they!—anyhow is there a better explanation why he had a heart attack out of the blue? There she's been, weekend after weekend, and she's this sexy Dane. Also your grandfather's *sort* of famous isn't he?—why shouldn't she decide to collect him! So, making love Fridays Saturdays Sundays *and* the mornings maybe, at his age? Hoh!"

The grandson was decently silent.

She was amused.

"Oh what would you do without me to tell you things?" she teased him. "Oh Richard *think* if I turned you loose."

He shut his eyes. And seemed to turn away, scowling.

"Oh my, are you sulking at me?" she giggled.

He was silent.

"But poor sweetie *listen*," she told him, humoring him, "I don't think anybody's prettier than you do I? Except of *course* I'll have to turn you loose some time, why won't you see! And suppose my out-of-her-mind sister leaves Charles? Richard I *told* you!"

He opened his eyes, speechless.

"Well don't glare at me, goodness!" she cried.

"But *jesus*, Mimi, your own sister's—"

"But what if the complications are exactly part of what I ought to learn about, how do I know! Including learn how I can be sure I feel how I am—I mean I'd *know*, here, who Charles would be comparing me with. As of course he would—they always tell about their others, so you have a norm. And anyway what *is* it like, at my age, with an experienced man, do you just blissfully lose your head?"

He was silent; he could have been stunned by his doom.

"Well you think about others than me don't you, so what are you glooming like that at me for!" she protested, reasonably. "Like when I first knew you you had an absolute *dog* for that sexy English instructor you have."

He muttered something.

"Well had you or hadn't you? You told me she was what your grandfather calls a 'dish,' it was one of the archaisms I *started* my generation-gap glossary with. Hoh, and you asked me what I thought she did for sex, you *do* have a voyeur-y mind!" she giggled. "And about faculty, *my!*"

He was silent.

"I bet you still think about being in bed with her, too, don't you!" she mocked. "And then you get all upset and stupefying about me and Charles—oh god, *men!*" she denounced him.

He snarled *hell* with Charles!!

"Oh cheer *up!*" she cried. "All I'm saying is if you *want* her why not go *after* her! you can't just spend your *life* letting girls seduce you like your mother's friend!—can't you for once act like a couthie?"

He shut his eyes again. She watched him, yawning.

And presently collapsed lazily prone, head on her arms, gaze on him still, as pondering his case.

But abruptly, "Oh but *listen!*" she yelped, and came up onto her pretty elbows again, laughing happily down at him. "Hey, what if I set her as a project for you!—like remember Mme. de Merteuil did for the Chevalier in *Les Liaisons Dangereuses?* So shall I give you till exams to seduce her? oh or at any rate *get* yourself seduced," she indulged him, "and if you won't give me your word of honor to *seriously* try I'll never sleep with you again? Well don't *glare*, why shouldn't you? I could help with suggestions and instruc—"

But he bellowed, "Mimi-jesus-goddammit-lay-*off!*" and bounded out of their bed and slammed off into the kitchen, where he flung open the refrigerator door with a crash into apparently the counter, and began banging its contents out onto the counter too. "You want a goddam beer?" he yelled.

Mimi rolled over onto her back, and thought. ". . . Not if that white wine's cold," she called, finally.

"Well fucking *okay* then!" he snarled, and rummaged.

But Mimi, lying there, was now lightly pedaling the air with delicious legs, a ghostly bicycling, smiling at their slim beauty as she counted to fifty.

". . . Mme. de Merteuil," she murmured. And started another fifty, giggling, as her scowling charge came hulking in with her wine.

12

Mrs. Tench-Fenton (looking heavenly) had come to visit Scrope so early, the morning he'd been trundled back from intensive care to a monitored room again, that she floated in to perch tenderly on his bed and flutteringly kiss him before the scandalized student nurse had half finished taking his blood-pressure and temperature, in fact the thermometer was still stuck in the helpless man's mouth.

So, for decorum's sake, she soothed the child's shock: "Oh sweetie Mr. Townshend and I have been married off and on for twenty years, goodness!—not of course *all* that often to each other, but I've been taking his vital signs since for any practical pur-poses he had any, *long* before I expect you were even born (not that vital *signs* are what one goes by with him!), in any case I'm only rushing past with this pot of caviar for the poor man—*will* you, like the lamb you look, just put it in a, oh careful it's heavy, in haven't you a refrigerator on the floor? so there won't be trouble about trays? and tell them he likes to eat it right out of the pot, just *it*, with a dessert-spoon, anyhow he hasn't the slightest fever, has he," she announced in a happy voice, and laid her lips lingeringly against his temple to make sure, "*perfectly* normal, and from his look what's his blood-pressure—his splendid hundred-and-twenty-over-eighty as usual?"

This loving rhetoric however, the nurselet gone, it appeared merely amused him: 'off and on' thank God of course *yes*, but that 'married' of hers?—that 'to each other' disingenuously slipped in as if grammatically connected? . . .

She said smoothly but had he ever seen much point, either, in disillusioning young people before they save you trouble by doing it themselves?—and when anyway she and he might very easily, as he was well aware, have *been* married, it came to the same thing. So how silly. Besides, what made him think he'd ever asked her to marry him all that often!

She didn't call hundreds of times often?

"Oh sweetie what difference whether how often, it always you'll notice seemed to be when I was already married to some-one you must perfectly well have known I wasn't at the time *dreaming*, even, of exchanging for you!"

She mean one of those semi-disposable bastards she claimed she adored almost as much?

"Are you insane?" she cried. "I did adore them!—him!"

Which them/him was this—that Siena time?

But "Oh Scrope how can you!" she rebuked him, now in it seemed a voice of tears. "How can you carp and cavil and *upset* me so, just when what have I been able to even think of from the first horrifying instant I heard they'd rushed you here dying, if not night and day worry about you, are you *heartless*? And just *back* from intensive care! and when even Sibylla was hardly al-lowed to visit you what *could* I do but wonder whether I might actually not ever see you alive again! I was so despairing I finally, oh well doesn't one *need* magics sometimes? I carried all your

novels into my bedroom and spread them on my bed, as if somehow they'd—oh Scrope I spent till *dawn* rereading all those
haunted places that are really about you and me, in tears over
them for you, half the time, you sounded so alive in them and
like how I remembered you were when what happens in them
happened, that I could almost feel you still *were* alive, till about
five o'clock I rang up the hospital, and they were *furious* at me at
such an hour but at least they admitted no you hadn't died."

He said, sounding moved too, well she was a sweet.

"Yes but then what I'd *found*," she said in a different tone
altogether, "was have you *any* notion how disorienting some of
those passages can be for me? for instance that girl in remember
the scene upstairs at Fouquet's where the man taking her to
dinner is you?—he says was that damn' waiter looking down her
dress (remember?) and naturally she laughs (well you sounded
so stuffy!) and says, 'Oh pooh, don't you think it's spiritually good
for his vanity to catch glimpses of what he can't have? but of
course *you* may!' which is *exactly* what I said, I never do know
what perfectly private remark I make to you may not turn up in
some context I've no control over! yes but then *later* in this novel
he takes what you *say* is this same girl to dinner at the Grand
Véfour, and she is en grande tenue, she's wearing this apparently
heavenly yellow silk evening dress and *long* black kid gloves
almost to the shoulder, and when the maître d'hôtel has seated
them she looks appraisingly round, table by table, and then
serenely settles back, politely smirking, and says, 'How nice, I'm
the best-dressed woman in the room, alors bon, qu'est-ce qu'on va
manger?' and takes the carte from the hovering waiter pour com-
mander, except sweetie *I* was never at the Grand Véfour with
you *ever!*"

He said huh? *wasn't?* nonsense!

"And I hardly ever wear yellow. So you see? there at three in the morning your memory of me was partly heaven-knows-which of your other girls, that flittering little Tory Bingham for all I know, and you don't think *that* was upsetting? And after their delicious dinner of I forget *how* many courses they were going dancing in some Montparnasse cellar you knew about except in the taxi they decided to go back to her apartment and make love instead! can't you *see* what a heartless outrage it is when this man, who *is* you— Well was I to think it was *me* in your arms or whatever girl your lecherous memory had grafted on to me! Or should I just thank Heaven (I suppose you'll say!) you at least aren't the kind of novelist who thinks the way to write love scenes is an exhaustive listing of everything including push-ups he imagines can go on in bed?—oh *dear* what mightn't I turn cold finding this helpless half-me reported as doing!" she ended, laughing.

But good god she knew as well as he did that a character wasn't who this or that enchanting aspect of her came from: the point was always the rightness of the detail *for* the character, not its provenance. Which was irrelevant.

"But it *wasn't* me. So who was it?"

Dammit he said look, in a long and spendthrift life how many expensive girls *mightn't* a man end up having fed at the Grand Véfour? did you keep gentlemanly count? Could've been any girl who felt he should be dressed full-fig for, to dazzle. Tory Bingham included. Except also (he added, reasonably) he could have made the scene up altogether. You often had to, real girls not always meeting specifications.

"Hoh!"

Look, why not sit on the bed instead of that damn' chair she was in?—she have to go *on* acting like the loveliest natural coquette a man had ever crossed himself in awe at finding in his arms?

This invitation was however so clearly irrelevant to any situation not long past and gone that she paid no attention to it beyond a forbearing brief smile, indeed at once she looked almost grave.

"No but Scrope love," she told him in a voice of concern. "I of course above all came to make sure for *myself* you were as much better as they said, but *also* to ask whether— Well by any chance has your lovely Sibylla, or my dear have *you* by any chance thought that just recently, oh dear how shall I put it? but I mean are they d'you think all *right*, Scrope, those married two of ours?"

The father uttered a cry.

"Oh sweetie then something *may* you've noticed be wrong?— or going wrong! Oh *dear*, because all I'd thought (which after all could of *course* have a perfectly innocent explanation) was that wasn't it a little odd of *her* to be bringing me that article of Charles Ebury's?—when it wasn't the one *Charles* and I had had such fun discussing anyway? And then, well, it was this very funny but Scrope *unkind* job on modern poetry, which is what my poor stepson her husband writes! And then she rather went on about *how* witty the article was. And how wonderful also he was being about this libretto of hers—which began to sound like a theirs! in short my dear *all* the happy signs not to say the stigmata! And, well, goodness, simply *Charles* then! heavens *how* easy to find one has a béguin for him, five years younger and I might well have waved myself under his nose myself! Are you listening to me or aren't you!"

"But what cockeyed scenario's this—*whose* béguin?" he as

good as gobbled at her, as if foundering. "*I* was given to believe, and not long ago, that *far* from its being what you appear to imagine, my daughter and your darling Charles, the *actual* trouble is she's got it in her lovely head Alec's been rolling in the hay with her dearest Amy good god—and Amy, poor child, came to me frantic!"

This naturally left them staring at each other, blank.

"In particular," he said finally, "she said how does one demonstrate *any* negative, innocence included. A dilemma one shares!"

"But they *are* innocent?"

"I have been seeing life steadily and seeing it whole till I am black in the face," he said grandly, as if quoting himself, "but how am *I* to know!"

So she appeared to weigh this.

And presently, "No but sweetie whichever way it *is*," she pointed out, "it doesn't *preclude* Sibylla's falling in love with Charles anyway, surely? And she *is* just as easy for a man to have a béguin for as—"

"Dammit," he cried, wretchedly, "d'you have to tell me!"

"But my absurd old *darling*," she cooed, "you *know* that these young people—"

"What's that got to do with *my* daughter! I've got nothing against young people, good god! Except their youth. Nothing against that either unless they overdo it. But are you suggesting that I can any day now expect the damn' fellow to come round dans les formes and ask the hand of my daughter in adultery?"

"Did you ask my fierce black-balling father for mine?"

"But goddammit *I loved you!*"

This so amused her that she came and sat on his bed after all. "And Charles doesn't adore her?" she teased him.

"Ah but why my sweet Sibylla?" this responsible father

snarled. "Why can't the damn' marauder take one of his students to bed with him, what are students for?—instead of *this* kind of disorder!"

"Oh but old darling!" she laughed.

"Something funny goddammit in a parent's wanting a darling daughter in good hands?"

"Wasn't *I*?" she said, and reaching a hand, stroked the inside of his wrist with the tips of remembering fingers.

So, "Ah, well," he conceded, with sentiment, "will my fingertips ever forget a sweet inch of you either? No, but how explain any of us anyway?" he ended, smiling back at her.

"You mean you were always it seemed married to somebody any time I happened not to be?" she said, tenderly.

"That had nothing to do with *us!*"

"Oh had it not!"

"My blessed woman," he besought her, "hasn't it ever occurred to you that one of *the* bonds of long and happy understanding between us mayn't well be that simply we find it natural to be in love with two people at once, provided one of them is the other of *us*? It's what we did!—what's more, if everybody else did too, don't we privately think la condition humaine would be as happy a state as ours has been? Dammit, if I ever decide to rearrange the past with an autobiography, I'll say so! (By the way, I've a splendid title, *Bygones, Begone!*) Ah though, Laura, think! —if we'd married each other would we have stayed as faithful as can't you see we've in fact been, unmarried?"

"I suppose what you're trying to convince me of is would we ever have found anybody as suitable as ourselves to be unfaithful with! And you tout *that* as an example for humanity?—and when you were just now fretting about our children's unhappy behavior? goodness!"

All he'd meant was—

"Which reminds me, Sibylla is in something of a fuss my dear about *you*, I don't know of course whether I'm supposed to tell, but there's this I'm informed rather *sexy* Yale creature you've acquired."

'Acquired'! Good *god!*

"Well everyone is at least *wondering* about the status."

Girl researching him a 'status'? Simply there was this book she was doing! About a couple of poets too. *The Creative Habitat;* not a bad title at all. Or anyway for a university press.

"But sweetie isn't there a certain ambiguity in the—"

At the start by *god* there was!—'d've taken any man in his right mind aback! Hadn't they told her? Because how did he want his sexual aspect stoodied, should she interview his mistress? Or had he groupie-type fans, like poets. Or naturally she could stoody him herself—'I sleep with this other poet while always I stoody him.' So help me, *that* it seemed was how the fellow'd found out he wasn't so gay as he'd led himself to believe ('Ho, so fonny!'). So what methodology did he prefer? For herself, 'A little I like better with girls,' but she was without preconceptions. But mightn't she mix them up—or wasn't she sleeping with the poet now? 'Naw, why. I finish to stoody him.' Dammit she was a study in herself! An *affair* with her?—Sibylla was out of her mind!

". . . So then who did she interview about you?"

There being nobody, *nobody!*

"You hadn't *any* current girl?" she cried, in shock.

So he reached for her, laughing at her: she think he'd have handed her over to the quantifications of sociology if he'd had?

". . . Not even a temporary one?"

No!

"But in prospect, surely?"

No, dammit, nor in prospect!—was he to pry into God's classified intentions? Some years, apparently He was principally interested (as by god why shouldn't He be!) in providing him with an effortless flow of His best syntax and vocabulary. But, other times, He saw to it, instead, that some delicious young woman stunned his mind blank by falling in love with him. Well, he was grateful for both these divine accommodations, how not! but he felt a pious diffidence about conjecturing, in advance, which accommodation he was about to be grateful for.

So, with one topic and another, Mrs. Tench-Fenton so over-stayed the permitted visit that she was rebuked with a severe and bureaucratic "But Mrs. *Townshend!*" by the nurse who here came in to end it.

13

Amy Hallam rang up Alec Urquhart, about this time, to fret oh what was she to do?—was her subconscious *obsessed?* All it was letting her think of, as plots, were idiotic real-life adulteries she knew about, and she was frantic!

"—like my by-marriage aunt who dumped my perfectly good uncle and went off to Antibes with a publisher? He was rich and easily dazed, so she married him and began to write books about genteel French eating, chefs it seems adored her, recipes and all. But then everybody's eating went genteel, so she wrote about being adored by the petit personnel generally, as well as chefs— *you* know, adored like Hemingway? And *told* the way Hemingway told how the Spanish petit personnel adored him, with subordinate clauses explaining how fine and true. And how the Italian adoranti adored him when he was in Italy. Though the Swiss, it seems, not. Of course Charles says, 'Do we have to justify some imputation of Jamesian seriousness to be thought a serious writer?—if the air of unreality fits, put it on.' But in real life she's married five times—does that mean she's very sexy or just not very sexy?"

Urquhart it seemed found no real reason to comment.

"Then did I ever tell you about a Texas classmate who's been sleeping weekends, in Walla, with a lout who heaves groggily out of bed before dawn Mondays and drives two hundred miles home to Crabtree, in Arkansas, where he lives with his regular girl? Well this is, I suppose, sort of extreme Texas behavior, but they do have universities and psychiatrists in case, anyway his name's Lance but she calls him Dick from having said 'For Richard for poorer' once about his ex-wife's alimony, and she's been having this affair for a *year*. But then one Sunday a little while ago he just got into his car and took off after breakfast—like that! Well, she thought what of it, c'est plus moi qui courrai après, like Zazie's mother; but then as the day went on she began to get into a rage, by evening she was pacing round *hitting* things with a quirt he'd given her, and finally about two in the morning she just blew *up!* and leaped into her car and roared off the whole preposterous two hundred miles through the night to his house in Crabtree (by then it was dawn) and began beating his flimsy door in with a tire-iron, shouting everything she thought of him and the slut he was in bed with at the top of her voice, oh *Alec* how sad! So he had to come down and let her in (his girl jumped out a window at the back and fled screeching), and she charged in and the first thing she saw was a beautiful little Sheraton chair she'd given him, so she beat it to flinders with the tire-iron, he hovering round bleating for Christ's sake what *was* this? till she charged through into the kitchen and flung open the cupboard doors and systematically *one by one* smashed every plate dish cup saucer bowl mug and glass into pieces on the floor! Then, as a sort of final *there!* she hurled the tire-iron through the glass of the door onto the patio and marched back into the living-room, where Lance was now sitting helpless on the sofa, and said, 'May

I use your phone?' and rang up her analyst back in Mt. Pleasant and talked for the better part of an hour, while Lance made breakfast. Oh Alec *so* sad somehow, and now Charles doesn't want me to visit her!"

This scenario Urquhart appeared to have no comment to make on either.

"Charles says on a *rational* plane it's of course easy to be cynical about women, but think how much easier it is for women to be cynical about men. Except what is the matter with the sweetie? Or is it just Sun Belt tastes in men. Are you listening to me, Alec? you're so quiet!"

He remained so.

"Oh but I *mustn't* keep you! Oh you are so sweet to listen to me going on and on wondering *why* it is whatever it is has so totally— And when it's *both* our woe! And nothing to be done anyway! Oh *sweet* Alec if only we could go to bed and *console* each other for their unfounded suspicions! D'you know, I'm in such a state I lie awake wondering has God perhaps done this to me for writing *nice* stories about unfaithful girls?—and with my darling Charles quietly sleeping right there beside me!"

So, shortly, she rang off.

14

<hr>

▼

Sibylla having said perhaps Charles *not* (for whatever reason) Les Piérides, it turned out it was the packed and stylish uproar of Five-Four-Three's noontide bar he eventually waited a good half-hour for her to arrive angelically on time in, eyes smiling into his as placatingly as if she were late.

So he kissed her cheek there in greeting but at once took her out of that jeweled din, in to their table, up to which the sommelier immediately trundled a wine-cooler and set to work on the cork, leering courteously.

At which evidence of foresight and sensibility, "But champagne?" she cried, as in bliss. "Oh but Charles how agreeable and fond!"

Had to lure her somehow, he said, and smiled, from this habit she'd got into of feeding her father lunch, how was the poor man today?

"And all iced and ready! Well, oh, but Pa? oh dear he's I'm afraid so much better he's in a fume at not being let go home— so difficult. Then it seems when my sweet mother-in-law comes to see him she upsets the nurses! You by the way," she added, in no particular tone, "he says she sounds like getting one of her lovely béguins for!"

He said what nonsense, eye on the sommelier's ballet—simply she was trying to coax fifteen hundred words on Ovid's *Amores* out of him. But they weren't letting Scrope go home *yet* surely, were they?

"Well Charles 'coaxing' is hardly the word that Daddy— No but what about your Mr. Molehill piece I took her specially?"

Turned down, he said amiably.

"Oh but Charles why!"

Her readers didn't apparently read. Or so she said.

"You went to *see* her?"

Here however the sommelier, beaming, poured their champagne. So this ritual they had to watch, silent.

But then, "To your Pa first anyway?" Charles said, and she said soberly, "To Pa," and they sipped.

"How's he putting up with lunch though without you?" he asked. "Nurses dish him up some sad dietician's gruel?"

"But I took him a salade niçoise, what d'you think!"

So they sipped again, smiling.

"I was thinking about him, waiting," he said then. "Or anyway about that *Town & Country* piece of his last year about a man and a girl meet by chance one day in town. Same Connecticut suburb set; same parties; always *look* for each other at parties. But always of course at parties other people there, and *this* day, into this restaurant he's having lunch alone in, she happens to come, by herself too."

Here however the maggiordomo interrupted with polished hoodlum mondanità, to demand their every wish. So, with the usual irrelevances (what was this 'cotriade'?) they composed their courses.

And as the fellow took himself at last off, here came the sommelier again, bowing, to pour.

And then to submit the wine card, for the signore's amiable decisions.

So then in due course:

—in she comes, alone too, and naturally he stands up and waves, and she threads her way laughing through the crowded tables and joins him. And after the smiling banalities of coincidence and amusement, and a sherry's been fetched her, and she's ordered, all at once it strikes the man—her it had struck the moment she saw him—that this must be the first time in all the vanished months they had known each other that the two of them had been—that extraordinary word—*alone*. He blurts it out—

"Oh dear."

"—well, yes, without thinking, but he does, and in the wordless moment of pause that follows (as your father put it) they gaze at each other, and the knowledge of what has happened is so shared, so tangible, it is like a third presence there between them."

". . . Oh Charles," she said.

"Well my lovely thing it *happens!*"

But she only gazed at him, as if helpless, silent.

"And what your father said," he finished, "is, suddenly they're free to say things to each other that are so new they can't even predict what they may turn out to be."

This she of course instantly deplored.

"No but Charles," she cried, "but that's only the way he—I mean oh *poor* Pa don't you think? because such an incorrigible romantic! Oh dear what am I to— Are you like him? Or do I mean goodness-are-you-like-him!" she more or less implored him, trying it seemed to laugh.

All *that* bad?

"Well but think how difficult for his girls—if only what they've had to live up to, heavens! Charles I'm in *awe* at Laura, handling it—and through three or four of their affairs, oh Charles the mere *times* before, the crescendo of it, how possibly could any woman— What are you looking at me like that for?" she faltered, in a voice suddenly near tears.

—Ah how do you coax them out of these equivocations, these immemorial temporizings?—and the sheer skill they do it with! He was bemused.

In fact reduced to mere sound—a baffled "Sibylla, *Sibylla . . .*" though whether reproach or caress had he any idea either? "My sad angel what *is* this!"

She gazed at him as in some wordless misery, gulping.

"*They*'re what we came here to talk about?—Laura and your father? . . ."

". . . I know."

"When all this time it's what's happened to *us*?—in God's name are we going to go *on* not saying it?"

"Oh Charles," she mumbled, as if despairing.

"What else on earth have I been able to think of, all these heart-shaken irrecoverable days you've known it too," he accused her tenderly, and slid a hand, palm up in simple entreaty, across the table to where, by her glass, lay hers,

Which however she had instantly to withdraw to her lap, for that sommelier once more loomed beside them, as in triumph presenting for approval the Montrachet the signore had had the spendthrift good taste to command; and now he slid it deftly into the wine-cooler beside the Moët, draped a spotless serviette across from rim to rim, and, bowing efficiently, whisked himself away.

These displays did however give them time to recover enough from what they had said to be able to deal with it.

At least provisionally.

The proviso being, for the moment, that what had happened had not so to speak all that *much* happened.

At any rate she now said, "Oh Charles . . . ," only a little breathless-sounding. "But then I have to find out about you, oh sweet," she put it off, in happy misgiving.

"Find *out* I adore you?" he cried, as if stunned at her.

"Oh but can't you see?—do I even know what questions to ask! Or anyway I suppose I mean questions you could reply to the way I want you to," she murmured, abashed. "Well, and because nothing like this has ever—oh Charles never like *this*, so am I supposed to *ask* are you what Daddy calls a marauder? Because are you? Only then suppose I mightn't find you so attractive if you a little weren't! And your feeling like this about me—well, so *touching* of you, Charles, as well as all the other lovely things it is, can't you see?"

So, like a man of sensibility (marauding or not), at least one preliminary query he at once answered, and as if in reproach at her thinking she need ask it: "But my *blessing* it isn't as if we were going to jump ship!—either of us."

She said, faintly, ". . . oh."

"But what's this 'oh'?" he teased.

"Well I *said* I had to find out!" she justified it, dolefully. "And now oh *sweet* Charles see what it is we're even this much doing! —meeting about it! and you won't tell Amy we did and I won't tell Alec—oh *already* who we trust is just each other? Oh I don't *want* any!" she fretted at the waiter, who was just spreading a crimson skiving of prosciutto over the cool greens of her melon. "Oh well then *yes* I suppose I do, yes leave it, *leave* it!" she countermanded, as in sheer distraction. "Oh Charles why didn't I order moules, like yours!" she mourned.

He of course said but God bless, take his!—melon'd suit him *just* as—

But she cried, "No but *how* am I to tell how I'll simply *feel*, if! I mean about myself, feel—I *know* how I'll feel about my darling Alec, I've as good as felt it about him for days haven't I? and how I'll feel about Amy—and feel I suppose won't I on your account as well as my own, oh *how* do these things happen!"

He said, lightly, " 'Happen'?" watching the waiter ladle his mussels from tureen to dish (the fidelity of the raven having no explanation either).

"Well does one get used to it, the feeling? . . . Or isn't it a question to ask? Only oh dear I'm *not* prying, but have you ever loved Amy and somebody else too like this—if you do me really? Or has the other one been just one of your students. And so sort of didn't count? Oh I *shouldn't* ask oh Charles forgive me? all these *low* shameful questions—and so jealous-sounding, when I'm not!"

"But my lovely Sibylla," he implored her, as if mildly scandalized at all this. "*Angel* will you stop!—making me miserable too! What *is* this fuss!—it isn't as if we suddenly love Amy and Alec in the least the less!"

"So you mean we *would* have to be utterly hole-and-corner wouldn't we, oh it sounds so dreadful, said like that! And how can we, Charles—I love Alec, I *do*! so why don't I seem to have the proper scruples I thought I did? All I seem to want to do this instant is *touch* you!" she cried, as in sad exultation. "Do you realize? we never have!"

"You've thought of that too!" he said, as if amazed.

"Oh darling yes!"

"Always some damn' Æschylus present!"

"So *that's* why you went on about Daddy's first-time-alone man and girl! Hoh, and looked so dark and brooding when I came in!—you were thinking up all your low persuasions?"

"Oh god," he said, "I was sitting there thinking of all those wasted months we'd known each other and said nothing— *nothing!*—how many hundreds of times I'd come into a room and you were there, and in my innocence all I'd thought was what a part of the pleasure I have in being alive you were—the instant lilt of delight through my senses no more defined than that! Can you imagine? So there in that shouting bar I sat, astounded at myself. Then in you came, so lovely I was dazed all over again, and I thought—"

"Ah but sweet," she interrupted— But here once more the sommelier appeared beside them. Where, with ritual gestures, he uncorked and poured the signore's Montrachet.

"Champagne *and* burgundy, goodness how lovely!" Sibylla murmured, watching. "Except Charles how disingenuous and disarming, you *are* planning to seduce me!"

This however being a charge one can neither honorably deny nor concede the truth of (or that calls for answering when moot), he merely snorted.

"Or just shouldn't I put it that *way?*" she teased, as a bus-boy began taking their empty plates. "And anyhow isn't 'alone' what one anonymously is, in restaurants?—ah mais comme c'est *bon*

que de pouvoir dire n'importe quoi sans se méfier qu'on n'écoute!"
she added, as if French were a foreign language, for their waiter
had arrived, chafing-dish and all, and was setting about the serving of their lobster, with its Marguéry counterpoint of contrasted
sauces, port and cream.

But what if they do listen!—"Ah, sweet," she said, "how long
have you known . . ."

" 'Known'!—when good god I've hardly even let myself believe it was happening?"

"Oh but *how* didn't you! Oh but I suppose how does anyone
start, simply I just began thinking about you, was all. After do
you remember our next-to-last Æschylus session?—Charles right
in the middle of it, how *didn't* you notice! suddenly I just over-
whelmingly wanted to touch you. . . . And of course I was so
shocked I—because what *was* this!—I looked up at you and, well,
I saw it was the lovely way you were looking at me that I must
be responding to. But then the shock was, the *way* I had
responded!"

"So that was it," he said. "My heart stopped."

"And then Charles the other day. When I phoned you. Because oh dear you knew as well as I did what we were as good
as saying."

But here, as the waiter began serving them ("*Très* chaud,
madame!"), the maggiordomo loomed up across from the fellow,
in liturgical supervision. So they watched.

But finally ("Now may I in God's name have this lady to
myself?") they could eat.

And did.

So, in due course, "Ah Charles *so* delicious," she told him.
"Will you always adore me with food like this?"

Appeal to her idealism mere matter of principle!

But this she was it seemed too murmurous with Montrachet to answer. Even lost in dream, for instead, "Oh blessing," she breathed, eyes in his, "where would you take me, to make love? Take me I mean 'if' oh sweet. Pa used to say girls seemed always to want to be taken to Venice. But why?—just the Byron in him?" she giggled. "Oh but then Laura always wanted Siena didn't she! d'you suppose it was because Siena was where they began, way back then, and she wasn't even my age? and so Siena was a sweet nostalgia for her? Oh darling where would you take me, to re-member?—if I mean we did stop being an if?"

So as who could say which way she was deciding, he said, why, in an ideal irresponsible world, he'd take her to Rome.

"Is that where you took Amy?"

He said, amused, "But Amy wasn't somebody else's wife."

"Oh Charles what a *heartless* thing to say!—and anyway didn't you take her anywhere? Oh how unfair! And when you'd taken her away from that perfectly sweet young—who *have* you gone to Rome with?"

Never with anybody. Look, just he *liked* Rome, was all. And its unlayable Classical ghosts—Ovid's Propertius's, all their sweetly strolling girls' in their summer dresses, tot *milia* formosarum!

But "Oh then but you and I Charles?" she lamented. "Rome or anywhere?—oh how *wouldn't* it be noticed we were both miss-ing at the same time. . . ."

Fatal, yes, he conceded. And saddening.

"Then what *do* lovers do about their wives and husbands—serious lovers! Can it always be as heart-breaking and impossible as this? Or oh dear am I sounding as delinquent already as my darling awful Pa!" she mumbled, in a happy voice. "And Charles

even if I were going to be! Oh my love have you thought even
where, if?—because *not* some horrid hotel, like your students!"

Ah, well, he said, logistics logistics—anyway other people's
rendezvous who knew! No, but for him, he said, and now he
reached across their table for the tips of her cool fingers, which he
coaxed with his own—but for him, would she forgive him? as a
man who—and hadn't she just now said who did they already
trust beyond each other!—would she, like the angel she was, forgive his having treated the mere desperate hope she might love
him as a working hypothesis for if she did? Because the university
ran an exchange, for senior faculty, and if you wanted to sublet
your apartment during a sabbatical to a responsible colleague or
visiting professor, you put it in their hands.

So, foresight being foresight even if only hope, a month ago
he'd begun asking whether—"But *angel* what's wrong!" he cried
out (startling that sommelier, who again was about to pour)—
for she was staring at him as if in terror, eyes enormous.

"But my darling woman," he protested, "even with the end
of term near we've a choice—including a small pied-à-terre in
walking distance in East Eleventh!"

". . . Oh Charles."

"Man in semantics's. His live-in poppet's decided to go to
Helsinki with him after all. Who *says* fidelity isn't what holds the
social fabric together! *Now* what's the matter?" he demanded,
amused. "Have I like a low swine taken away your last excuse?"

". . . But suppose I found out I love you more than I love Alec
—and then how would you feel either!" she mourned, seeming to
despair. "Or do you think I wouldn't even be wondering whether
I'd love you more if I weren't terrified I already do? Oh Charles
this is unfair I *know*, dithering like a—"

Here however that maggiordomo was again upon them, twin

bus-boys trundling the splendors of their laden chariots in his train, for which of his frutte and frivolezze and facezie would it please the signora/signore to expensively desire?

They stared at him, blank, stunned—for what was this, in what world?

But at last, ". . . Oh do we want desserts, oh Charles what are you having? oh give me I suppose a millefeuille thing then," Sibylla told the fellow, distracted, watching the bus-boy spring to life. "What *are* you having," she said mindlessly, for he had already pointed at a glistening tart, greengage it appeared. "—unfair I know, oh my poor sweet are you seething? But it's only that it's been so long I just *admired* you terribly, why didn't I ever think of 'unfaithful' as being such a solemn word!"

"But God in heaven what's my adoration then!" he teased. "Am I a man who loves you or just a mist before your eyes?"

". . . But Charles *is* this how one lives? It's I know how Daddy has, and perhaps you too? because I *haven't* asked—but is my generation like for instance Laura's, goodness! And how can a lover ever have been as simple as they can make it sound! So why do you think I can't decide!"

So again he was amused.

"Ah, dammit, Sibylla," he cajoled, "which side of this dizzy debate with yourself are you planning to end up losing!"

"And you're not even thinking practically about the risks of your wicked garçonnière!—and when not only would this colleague of yours know, but his girl!"

"Dear god," he said, "the poor bastard's a—"

"And have you even thought about my side of us?—do I know whether you seriously adore me at all!" she teased, and now she too was amused. "I'll bet if I asked you whether you love me more than you love Amy you'd say, 'How do *I* know, I've never been in bed with you,' wouldn't you!" she accused him, laughing. "Goodness why do I even consider you for a lover, all you want's an *answer!*"

So this went on.

Through their coffees and brandies, on. On into the long, murmuring, tenderly wrangling afternoon.

Undecided. Her father would have been scandalized.

—But at the end, as he handed her out of their taxi at her doorstep, ". . . But don't you Charles at least *think* I'm trying?" she conceded; and though she only let him kiss her angel cheek, for a moment she made it seem she was in his arms.

15

A day or so after this, Sibylla was allowed to fetch her father watchfully home.

As however he had to be accounted an invalid for a time still, Mrs. Tench-Fenton had said why shouldn't she send her excellent cook over, and one of her maids, to help make do—"because sweetie you know how he can be! so then this way you won't have to lift a finger, just be *there* with him, and of course go out any time too."

Also, for the first night or two (which who knew whether critical), as *she* had after all her handsome husband to see to, she herself would move in—night nurses or not, one never knew, he having been so frighteningly near death so *few* days before. There should be family! Or as good as.

(He remarked vive l'autant-que!)

But then where, he said wouldn't the question be, once he was well enough to recuperate—where would she consent to his talking her into going with him *to* recuperate? and this they were agreeably arguing about in his pantry, dressing-gowned for early bed this third night home, as they finished off the second bottle of their before-dinner Bollinger, with a white peach or so each from a bowl on the serving-table.

She was saying didn't he realize her editors' vacations were scheduled a *year* in advance? and at the moment the only editor she would think of deputizing even for his impossible two weeks, and exchange times with, was Tammie, and Tammie was expecting her stupid baby within the next ten days *besides* having these ghastly dismantling scenes divorcing its father (who said he wasn't). Anyway, anyone in Scrope's still perilous condition, when wasn't he practically tottering actually? how could he consider any such doctorless risk as the back-country isolation-from-everywhere of the Côtes-du-Nord out of season! the nearest even-for-France-modern hospital to Port-Blanc seventy kilometers of dreadful chest pains along that wild coast road to St. Brieuc not even in an ambulance, or for all he knew nothing but somebody's desperate passing Deux Chevaux! And for mere nostalgia?—was he *mad*?

He said but when it was *lovely* nostalgia?—and reached for her, coaxing.

And as they were in any case leaning amiably side by side against the pantry counter, she indulged him.

Anyway for the moment.

So then now at least, his arm lying lightly (transitionally, even) round her shoulders, they could argue in comfort.

So he said, tenderly, did she love him dammit or didn't she. Was he reduced to *reminding* her how once she had, and *at* Port-Blanc? Why else did she think he wanted the two of them to return, even if not specifically to that weathered grey gentil-hommière they'd rented then, on its low headland up from the sea, the scrolls and arabesques of lichen green-gold and black on the worn stone of its façade, and over the portico stone beasts and flowers carved, and stone crockets and even finials along the cornices—and the green ferny fronds of the bracken sloping up and away landward, so tall she'd teased him why not make love in them!

"Yes and you fussed about vipers! *Were* there vipers?"

He said god *yes!*—and the terrasse the salon's French windows opened out onto had a rose-granite balustrade, with vased turnings, and balustraded flights of stairs curved down through the thickets of bougainvillea and laurel and white bursts of hortensia everywhere to the blue circle of the sea beyond, and she remember the little oriel balcony the bedroom gave on? rose-granite too, and that first morning she'd woken early, not being alone—so early the first pale cool dawn quiet lay over everything still, and she had stepped out and leaned on the balcony railing and watched the sky turn slowly as deep a blue as the sea, until finally she had come back in and kissed him awake, and said high over the flowering headlands there was a kestrel soaring.

". . . so sweet," she murmured, head against his cheek. "And my dear that *freedom* of being alone."

Even the storms, he agreed, were a privacy: that savage tempête, that second week, she'd curled up by his knees before the fire, hail shattering down the panes, and written her letters.

"As I should've days before, goodness!"

". . . Which damn' béguin was it, Dominic?"

"Bart."

"Bastard off organizing that land-swindle in Damascus!"

"Beirut, sweetie, and he made a *great* deal of money with it. And it wasn't a swindle, I've still enough of his mètres carrés in Bliss Street for a bayt. No but my silly sweet, Port-Blanc?—it was back *then*, our Port-Blanc, you were a mere—"

"Ah Laura *look* dammit!" he complained, and shifted her

round to where he could see her properly. "Where could my health, if that's the argument, be in better hands? Brittany's our Bona Dea country, not that moralizing old metic Jehovah's! The Curia hasn't even jurisdiction in Basse Bretagne: St. Thégonnec and St. Efflam and St. Guénolé and St. Caradec and St. Tugdual are by god *working* saints there, what's Rome know! *Or* Canterbury."

For that matter (he said happily, for she had drifted closer, in amusement)—for that matter Who did she think had cajoled her into saying that heart-stopping Yes on that cockeyed balcony at Cacciapuoti's at the start of it all?

Or even, Who was it this *moment* having her nuzzle his collarbone so rememberingly?

So she drew somewhat away, smiling.

Though naturally what a relief (she said) if nothing else, to see him like himself again, even if so tiresomely like. Because how could even a man as lifelong spoiled as he was think reciting these lists of tender memories was all he had to do!—who was it used to quote that marquise of Musset's at her? 'quelques phrases bien faites, un tour de valse et un bouquet, c'est pourtant ça qu'on appelle la cour?' gently taking one of his hands away to put his glass in again. Because *also* things she remembered were the street fair by the cathedral in Tréguier that day, and that enchanting little fillette— She couldn't have been more than six, *beautifully* dressed (as was her young maman), little white gloves and all, and she'd been gazing so longingly at the booth where they were selling balloons that her mother said alors bon, what color had she decided on, "and oh Scrope *remember* how disdainfully she dismissed her plebeian yearnings?—'Mais j'aurais l'air de quoi, dans la rue, avec un ballon!' "

. . . 'd reminded him of Sibylla, little.

"Well sweetie what she reminded *me* of was *me!*" she told him, and simply in it seemed amusement, kissed him.

So he gratefully set his glass back on the counter and would have gathered her in again if "Oh but my old darling," she hadn't murmured, and gently stopped him, "after nearly dying before my *eyes* before I even knew, you expect to go *on* the same as ever? and when even your blessing of a Sibylla has time and *again* said to me, 'The trouble with dearest Pa is, all the women he knows are female.' "

"Look, blast it," he said, reasonably, "whose fault's that?—if a man has the sense to *like* women don't they behave the way he likes?—couldn't be simpler!"

"No my dear what I *meant* was," she said, as if this were so, and smoothing the lapel of his dressing-gown, which was not rumpled, "shouldn't we I thought try to deal with the *real* reality of what we've been to each other? Or do I mean 'are.' "

So he snorted. As if she hadn't said this, or something as out-of-character like it, every *other* time it had turned out they ended up concluding they couldn't resist each other that one more time either!

"Yes but sweetie *now* you've just had this dreadful monstrum of a— Oh why have you been such an unteachable marauder!" she grieved. "*Always* a marauder!"

He the marauder of them? he cried, amused—"you lovely flitting apparition are you pretending you don't remember the nonsense that it happens *led* to Port-Blanc? There on my doorstep at two in the morning—"

"It was *not* two in the morning! it wasn't even—"

"—blaming *me* for Bill Basset's stifling-past-endurance mind!"

"Well why had you wickedly *let* me marry him!"

"Good god, woman, was I to *stop* you?—for all I know you

need one of these damn' bel homme types now and then to remind you how disappointing they are."

"Are you self-satisfied past *reclaiming?*" she cried at him, in a
fume. "Or simply don't you *hear* how fatuous and smug about
other men's love-making you let yourself sound! If *that* was the
tone of that outrageous piece thank Heaven at least somebody at
Vanity Fair had the editorial sense, *and* enough concern for your
reputation, to reject it! Have you forgot the cloudburst of abuse
your arrogant *Esquire* piece brought down on you five years ago?
—over what you called 'the scandal a rosy mouth so often astounded and saddened you with,' oh *really* Scrope what a phrase!"

He said ah but dammit—

"Because husbands, you said, were of course no competition,
or all those nightlong darlings would never have been there in
your arms, telling you!—but were none of their incompetent
lovers competition *either?* . . . 'Girl after girl,' you boasted, 'the
soft reproaches were stored up in your memory'—your *detestable*
memory!—so what could a reasonable man conclude, amazed or
not, you said, but that hardly one lover in fifty was an improvement on even husbands, *oh* what simpering self-complacency!"
she finished, in a passion.

So for a courteous moment he considered this, as called for.

Though, then, well, yes, if she liked, how it could look, yes
he supposed (he agreed, peaceably); but the *fact* perhaps still
being he was a modest man? The immemorial trope was, all a
woman existed for was to fall in love, and the shocking thing was
so many still believed it. But take a calm, a Classical, view for
once: what amazed him, didn't she see? was an adorable woman
telling him she loved *him*—out of millions, *him?*—and this dammit was not just bred-in modesty but the observed fact that clearly
it never crossed the minds of a shattering percentage of the

women who bothered to look at him that he was anything to look at twice!

"Well you *are* hardly sweetie a bel homme are you!" she denounced him.

He said but he—

"And don't tell me I *know* you haven't had to be!"

All he'd meant—

"Will you stop *explaining!!* Must you go *on* about your indefensible misdoings like that great stupid prig of a Tolstoi making his fiancée read his diaries?—and spoil every *sweet* memory I have of you mingled in!"

So what was there but be silent.

She had even stopped looking at him.

For she stood there silent now too, gazing down it seemed at the fluted glass her hands clasped as in grave ritual before her, eyelids so vailed he could not see her eyes; she might have been an Attic *kora with kylix,* from the frieze of some ruined temple, of Artemis, or Roman Bona Dea, the long folds of her peplum motionless in time; a khoëphora, perhaps, though the tiny garlands of bubbles the champagne loosed endlessly upward from nowhere a libation to Whom?

And as it seemed things stood, what was he to say?—for was this a mere Laura dudgeon she was in, or was she done with him once for all *and* for ever, as on this or that occasion before.

At last, though (for in fact what else?), warily he stretched out his hands and took her waist in his fingers.

And as she did not move, ". . . all this head-tossing," he murmured, coaxing.

So at least she looked at him again, silent.

". . . Giraudoux de Manhattan not Tolstoi anyway," he said, and smiled.

"As if it isn't bad enough being in love with you!" she cried, "without having you carelessly tear my heart in two by nearly dying!"

But as at least the tone of this nonsense was relevant, he at once turned sober again.

And said, as if earnestly, but good god hadn't they from the first survived things infinitely more upsetting and disrupting than a mere cardiac fright? For two dispossessed years, after the summer they'd met ended, hadn't the whole damn' continent and sometimes the ocean too lain between them? *and* she'd acquired was it Bart? yet the instant—

"It was Dominic!"

Yet from the *instant* they'd once more been within—

"And you know yourself there never *was* a more entirely presentable bel homme—besides, so touching, Scrope, his starting that West Coast edition for me, was I to be mannerless and intractable? heavens! And at least Coasties by and *large*— Well it's *Texans* think they're normal, Coasties know better. So one simply revises a few assumptions, and you know as well as I do, that *first* summer of ours—ah, sweet, who had I ever had or imagined like you yes I *know*, but it wasn't the way it—the way we've—well I was only *light*-mindedly out of my mind over you, was all!"

Well Heaven of course defend him from controversy, he said amiably (and lifting one of her hands gently from her glass he kissed the cool inside of her wrist), but wasn't the way thank God they'd since come to feel about each other foreshadowed, by the time he'd sadly put her on her plane that final day?—like the scribbled note he found she'd tucked into the pocket of his next morning's shirt in the drawer, 'Un doux baiser, mon amour, et un bon retour de nos nuits,' and taking her glass from her other hand to set out of the way (and this she at least allowed) he gathered her in.

But she laid her fingers against his breast, between, if only as reminder.

And said, "But oh sweetie but Port-*Blanc?*" as in womanly or even in true concern for such folly, "when isn't what you in fact ought to have is somewhere they will look *after* you properly, recuperating? instead of just some curtseying gardienne to get you breakfast! Because if you sentimentally insist on Brittany I know this country-de-luxe place with 'de ravissantes dépendances' not fifteen minutes from remember Pont-Aven? that that Frenchman who was doing me our Étapes series took me to lunch at— well and to engagingly seduce me at he of course hoped too, *so* French to still think one goes to bed with a man because he was brought up thinking one's panting to—I thought in *1984* sweetie you're so hermetically French it has to be explained to you?— because *such* a pity when he really was very attractive—and did behave I admit very well, not only not sulking but hardly even downcast, in fact the only inconvenance qu'il s'est permise was a slight surprise that I could keep my fingers off him, I thought oh *dear* what does that say about French women! because can you imagine making love in that ambience? not only was the lunch very good indeed (and he ordered admirably) but I looked at the rooms of the auberge side of the place and they were *expensively* cosseting. Also, for the way you are about oysters, Belon is literally just round the corner! It's near this no more than village, Moëlan, but it's definitely *not* one of those summer fruits-de-mer establishments, *this* one's gorgeous fruits-de-mer salver had for instance oursins, and *no* dismal winkles, oh Sibylla would love it!" she finished, as if helpfully.

Which was as likely to be coquetry as disingenuousness.

So naturally this amused him: what under the sun had Sibylla to do with it!

". . . But sweetie weren't you I thought just a *tiny* bit worried about her?"

So he took her hands again, and mockingly rested a wrist on each of his shoulders. Which, this time, seeming to decide, she cautiously allowed.

"About Sibylla?" he protested. "My devious blessing do you want me to believe you think the way to keep my sweet daughter out of that damn' young professor's bed is to take her off from her husband's too?—and to a place with nothing for her to do in but listen to her dear father by day and merely *think* about making love half the night?—you, of all people? Look, whose rosy mouth d'you think it was that sweetly— Are you going to put your arms round my neck properly or are you practicing being a lovely statue of yourself?"

". . . I don't think this is good for you, is all."

"What in God's name's good-for-me got to do with it!"

"And not for your heart *either*, Scrope, the time it's become —and when you *know* the doctor said bed early! Oh are you going to be silly and overdo and harrow everybody who loves you all *over* again arguing about trifles?"

" *'Trifles'!*"

"But Scrope—"

"Not knowing whether you'll come or not, a *trifle?*"

". . . But suppose I lost my head over you *again!*" she put him off, in a voice it seemed near tears.

"Then come *with* me goddammit!" he implored her (for what's logic?), and slid his fingers lovingly up her slim back, in caress at last.

"But ah why don't you think of *me?*" she murmured, lost.

"When I good god *adore* you?" he laughed, and tilting her head in his fingers he kissed her, for some time.

Till she took her mouth away, sighing, ". . . so irresponsible . . . ," smiling into his eyes.

As (after all!) often before.

So, "Alors—à Moëlan?" he asked her, finally.

And at least, ". . . oh darling I'll *see*," she seemed to promise.

But then she reached carefully for her glass again. And shortly after this, early bed it was.

16

That afternoon, it happens, Mimi Hallam and Richard Scrope Townshend III had been celebrating, abed, their first three months of each other abed—this time, again, in 21 Blair, a suite now in fact part of their sense of the pleasures of a stable tradition, Richard having meantime discovered that his Great-Uncle Tom (Class of '31) had in his day not only roomed there but been caught with an improper girl there by the proctors, and resoundingly expelled.

Mimi had, besides, as an act of amnesty for the occasion, forgiven Richard's blundering into that English instructor of his's husband ("At least you found out what she does for sex!") and had added sentiment by wearing his shirt, unbuttoned, to make love in.

Academically however it had been necessary to bring her notebook ("Mais pour les relâches entre nos ébats, stupid, what d'you think!"), her term-paper being due in only four days more as it was.

So, now, kneeling up beside her dulled boy in their twice-tumbled bed, she was reviewing, for possible revisions of the final draft, her notes for Part II: Parameters.

"—so I don't care, I'm going to *say* there's no statable norm for a spectrum of presbephebic ambience imbalances, weighted for phyletic and era factors or not! Anyway even if your grandfather does seem to set a novel in 1959, *that* could be no more than what Professor Staling calls a 'preening factor.' So when you can't synthesize you *list*, so taaaah. Oh *anyway* the state Staling's in about me, I'll get an A, so what. Oh but listen, *here*'s this quote from your grandfather I told you I was thinking I'd epigraph the whole section with—

> This generation baffled him—psychotherapy-simple was what they were! Reliably informed by god they went to Central Park in groups Sunday mornings and solemnly threw stones to work off aggressions, you credit such a thing? And where'd they get the stones—Altman's? In *his* time what you did Sunday mornings was laze in bed with somebody delicious. And have brunch *late*. Though ah dammit how was one to pass *on* one's knowledge of the amenities, one's touch! The very technique was lost. So everything it seemed had to be learned over again, generation after generation to the fumbling incompetent end of time! Or like as not, *not* learned properly at all, and only the sad disillusionments passed on instead.

Well it sounds pathetic, but goodness it's not *us!* And Charles and Amy hardly get up Sundays at all. So who's disillusioned?"

He appeared to reflect.

"Who's this telling whoever-it-is off?" he said presently. "Grampa or some other lecturing old bastard?"

"Oh Richard it's a *character!* In a *novel!* It's this novelist who's being writer-in-residence at Bryn Mawr. And there is this dumb English-major who's been sleeping with him, so it's *her* he's talking about the generation gap he has with that I'm quoting in the *text* passage—

> . . . like the time he'd said to this demure and naked child (and in sheer awe, mind you!) he'd said *god* what a lovely piece she was!—and so help him, what had she done but go white with outrage, shriek 'So *that's* all you think of me!!' at him, and fling on her clothes and out his astounded door for ever! And in fact absolutely refused to sleep with him for a week.

Of course she did have a point—*all* the dictionaries say 'piece' meaning a girl is 'archaic or dialect.' "

So he thought this over.

. . . His *door* astounded?

"Oh Richard it's a *metonymy!* No but then I checked about 'piece' with Charles that night I spent in town, and he said ah, well, Scrope invents his own dialect, stylizing. Also anyway he *has* a lot of old-fashioned prejudices and behaviors, Charles for instance said Scrope claims courtship is every bit as productive an alternative as just saying *You wanna?* Oh it was lovely, Amy wasn't there, so I sat on their bed, and Richard he really *talked* to me! And he *isn't* three times my age, he won't even be thirty-seven till September, and we talked for hours. I asked him how professors feel when some student falls in love with them, what do professors, well, *do?* He said why? was I thinking about seducing one? I said goodness no!—the sort of professors we have at Princeton? my!—no, actually I was just asking what *he* did when a student began to behave as if she wanted him badly, I'd been taking this *course* that'd made me sociologically investigative. Because Richard I wanted to see whether he'd pretend it never happens to him. But of course he just looked mondain and amused, and said *'Do'?* what would any gent do! So I said, 'Oh but Charles not what anybody would, what *you* have,' so he began to laugh and said what was I doing, interviewing him? what kind of course I'd taken *was* this! Because in principle, or anyway *his* principle as an un-marauder, these things depended on your best honest estimate of how any given girl's temperament and experience would bear up under the assaults of your adoration, oh Richard he was a trance!"

Her bedfellow, it seemed sulkily, said nothing.

But she paid no attention. "Because Charles said look," she went on, serenely, "if a girl goes to bed with you to make sure she's as lovely as why *shouldn't* she hope she is—and he said that's always *a* reason, never mind all the silly others—then the only decent way to respond to this gift from Heaven is not just confirm her hope but dispel any last possible doubts she could *ever* have, and for good! So, when the affair's over, she not only has no regrets about herself and folly, she also ends up *fond* of you, and what more can a man want!—and he sounded so charming I didn't even point out how neatly *that* excused a man from responsibility! Though he says the average man never has *any* real idea what he has in his arms. Or how she operates, which is why the poor clod's hardly serious competition, oh Richard he was *telling* me about himself, imagine! But *now* what are you looking all grumpy and sullen for, I didn't *do* anything about him did I?"

". . . Well but *jesus*, Mimi!" he mumbled.

"And anyway, listening to Charles, I thought of something

to try for *you* Richard, making love. Oh god you look like that phrase Charles said your grandfather says is the style most novelists write their novels in, 'Henry shook his head thoughtfully'— shall I just give up? No but I was thinking how caressing Charles sounded on my tapes, with Amy, as well as how he *is*, so then I thought how Amy sounded, making love with him, oh Richard *the* most erotic *wildly* blissful little whimpering cries, goodness! and I thought I bet it would excite you too if *I* made them, because wouldn't it? But then I thought but does she do it on purpose, to excite him, or only because she feels so lovely she really can't help it—how *does* one get to know, about other women? What did that sexy friend of your mother's last summer do? Or were you I suppose too dazed by her to notice. No but then I thought but suppose Amy *is* consciously being blissful with Charles, then *oh* what a hypocrite when she's so wild about your uncle she's committing adultery with him! Unless, that is, she's still in total pieces about Charles too?—do you suppose you can actually be *in love* with two men at the same time? I mean goodness maybe there *are* still things to find out!" she crooned at him, exulting.

But her Henry did not even shake his head. Women being beyond us.

17

One morning that week Amy Hallam rang up Alec Urquhart and said could he perhaps did he suppose have been mistaken about Sibylla's suspecting them?—it having been actually mostly inference after all? Sibylla hadn't *said* had she? So what if perhaps she didn't think it either! And so Charles didn't either *either!*

Because, first, the adorable way Charles had recently—well she of course couldn't tell him in detail, but the way he'd been not just making love but oh *everything!* for instance just last night about *adultery* he was adorable, he'd said it was a branch of civilized deportment you had to *acquire* the traditions of, being unfaithful wasn't just something you did by light of nature, as between consenting illiterates, you had to read up on it, and would he joke if he thought?

"Because in particular, Alec, he said the first arms men end up in, as things go, are your wife's delicious best friend's or your own best friend's delicious wife's, so is light of nature going to prepare you for the hair-raising social legerdemain you're then stuck with? So, sweetie, would he have said 'your wife's best friend' when I *am?*" she ended happily.

He said um.

"And then, second, I don't see how otherwise Sibylla would have confided in me (as she just *has,* and for me to use for a story she even said if I liked) this anecdote about her father she has never told *anyone*—never even hinted how amused she felt about him sometimes because of, Alec! This was some year he'd been talked into at least *being* at this literary bash in Berkeley, and he'd said to her why not come by for a couple of days' cultural pub-crawling, he was staying with his editor's cousin, who'd be delighted to put her up too, so one afternoon she'd left Scrope lazing in the sun in the rose-garden behind and gone upstairs, and was standing at her bedroom window for a moment looking out at her father and thinking really how nice he looked for a man his age, when she heard this car turn into the drive and in past the house and it stopped by the gate into the garden right under her window. And Alec out sprang this *very* young wife, Sibylla said she'd it seemed only *graduated* at Berkeley the year before! of the brilliant young professor who was running the conference—and oh Alec Sibylla says she simply *raced* across the garden to Scrope and flung her arms round his wicked old neck, laughing in sort of pure joy, and the easy, *accustomed* way her father—well it was so absolutely in-*bed*-used-to I think Sibylla was even shocked! and then this girl took his hands and practically she said *tugged* him to her car, both of them laughing, and as they went past under her window Sibylla heard her exulting, '. . . and I won't have to go pick him up till after *eleven,* oh angel *think!*' and then they were gone. And Sibylla thought but she's hardly older than I am! and she was scandalized, maybe I would've been too. But then, later, she decided well but what a pleasure for him at what was he? fifty-five? so why not. So *there* is my age-difference story!—but with *two* girls of the same difference, so I'll tell it about one from the standpoint of the other and it's *perfect!* And then it seems Scrope upset a lot of people with a public lecture because he said academic criticism was salvos of stately clucking from the scenery, so I can make my older man intellectually controversial and sarcastic too. Also, Sibylla once told me he said Greek tragedy has screwed up literary theory *and* practice for the last twenty-five hundred years, by making solemnity the basic criterion. And Charles says Scrope is entirely right —if you don't make your characters suffer he says how are the boys in the back room to be sure what you're writing is Literature? so then they can't analyze it. He says William Gerhardi, who he says wrote the only Chekhov novel in English literature, said critics feel *uneasy* when a writer isn't solemn. As if comedy weren't serious!—he says for instance Scrope took Housman's

> Could man be drunk for ever
> With liquor, love, or fights

and rewrote it as comedy: 'a pretty girl within grabbing range, a dazing drink, and somebody to knock down,' and was that any the less *serious* writing?"

Urquhart said nn.

"Oh though doesn't it feel lovely Alec maybe not being suspected any longer? even if maybe we never all that actually were anyway! Hoh, and so *free*-feeling!—oh dear if I were still having that crush on you d'you suppose we'd—because it *would* be the perfect time, being I mean suddenly all *un*suspected! And when we've been so agonizingly through it all together already!

Or *do* you think. Oh *dear!* I mean I had this same situation in a story once, only in the story the girl ran off into the Peace Corps, and none of my magazines liked it. Oh Alec. I mean I *adore* Charles! And your students are sort of a groupie thing aren't they. So neither of us ever seriously of course—but then it wasn't a sensible way to end the story either, or d'you think."

He did not reply.

"And anyway it would be as heartless to make Charles and Sibylla suffer from our *having* an affair as we thought they were suffering from thinking we were when we weren't, oh Alec how can such things ever *happen* to people like us!" she wailed, and she might have been in remorse already.

But he was silent still. Not being all that ex cathedra articulate anyhow.

18

Mid-afternoon by now it may have been, beyond the shuttered windows, even it was late afternoon the drawn curtains helped muffle and close as if evening away, but their bed's tall hangings too Sibylla had loosed from the tester's ties, to swing down around, enfolding, so under that hooded canopy was dusk deep as secrets—even poised on an elbow there, close beside, she hardly made out among those nightfall shadows her lover's eyes.

Which presently it seemed it tenderly amused her were closed, anyhow she now drooped her enchanted head and kissed them, to open them.

So, amused too, he pulled her down. And for a time she lay there, nuzzling him as in sluggard happiness, lips grazing his shoulder, murmuring.

So that presently he murmured, ". . . what," in return.

But in that musing indolence of limbs she seemed too lost in mere contentment, or in dream, to reply.

So they dozed there, wordless.

Except that, at length, she stroked him, laggardly, a mere once, light palm dawdling along his thigh; in torpor; in lullaby.

". . . and so lovely," she whispered. Though of what this was, who knew.

But finally, ". . . even this place, lovely, oh Charles such luck!" she told him, and kissed his throat, for such blessings. "Because how not, you know, wonder. I used to come walk past, along Eleventh Street, some days two or three times past, before they turned it over to you, I'd look up at our third floor and think 'next *week* it will be ours . . .' and try to decide how I hoped the bedroom would turn out to be, and the bed, oh and us in it, but then sometimes my heart would *sink*, for what if it was in someone's *really* awful taste, because what kind of girls do semantics professors have?"

Needn't've worried, he said. Actually was what her father called a 'dish.'

"But then the heavenly day came and my darling it was *this!*" she exulted. "Oh and from the very first, lovely! . . . And *you* lovely, even the way you simply stood me by the bed and adorably undressed me, ah Charles I felt seduced dans les *formes!*—and to think at our lunch that day I'd been modestly wondering whether to ask, well, 'Are you . . . very physical?'—oh *dear!*"

So he began to laugh.

"*So* practiced and wicked of you!" she teased him. "Poor deprived sweet, have you always had to just dream of having a garçonnière?"

Brought up to have *some* ideals, dear god!—were there no goals to be set before a growing boy, to strive for and attain? No, but what was this 'practiced and wicked' she was disingenuously charging him with—*she* not experienced? Was that delicious delaying him with salvos of fluttering little interrupting kisses the whole time *not* a Special Occasion expertise that Ovid's Corinna herself—

"And you didn't like it?—hoh!"

Good god he'd *never*—!

"And anyway I *felt* like kissing you!—and never stopping ever, and touching you and touching you—and you call that 'interrupting'?"

Well, he said, you could *combine* efficiency with a—

But "Ah, sweet," she murmured, "when my fingers were beginning to learn you too? . . ."—so for some time, then, they said nothing more.

At last, though, she slid up from him, onto an elbow again, gazing soberly down.

And asked, as uncertainly as if it were not altogether a question, ". . . Have we perhaps my love do you think— What have I done to, well, to how you feel about Amy?"

As this could also however mean what *he* had done, to her feelings about Alec, he was warily silent, to see.

"Or shouldn't I ask."

Well, but she had.

So he said, as if lightly, feelings about Amy? when all he could feel was *her*?—what cockeyed time was *this* to ask! with not an atom of his body that wasn't shivering like a tuning-fork with delight in her! Couldn't she realize she'd obliterated every other girl he'd ever as much as glanced at—or that in the future he ever might? Yes, but was *that*, God help him, the way he would presently feel when he was clothed and in his right mind again? and she alas in hers, and in practiced decorum they descended their borrowed stairs, and then sedately down the front steps too, and like the well-brought-up personnes de condition they were set out as if for a Sunday stroll, not even holding hands! . . .

". . . Oh Charles," she mumbled.

"And wouldn't you have to say the same?" he asked her tenderly. "At this undeceived and lovely moment does it seem to you you'll ever again particularly want—"

"I know," she said dolefully.

"Then what?" he coaxed, and slid his fingers up her docile back, to pull her down to comfort and consolation.

But "Ah Charles so much to be endlessly wary about too?" she fretted, resisting. "And then all the feelings that—the edge-of-consciousness— Oh how do I say it? I mean do you sometimes feel, well, *odd* my darling about me, coming to you from you'll never perhaps feel quite sure what with Alec?"

But she didn't feel odd about him, with Amy.

"But you're my *lover*, heavens!"

He was amused: he wasn't Amy's too?

"Only then why doesn't it seem to count!" she lamented. "Or do I just put up with thinking about it because I love you so much?—because that time she had a crush on Alec I stopped even kissing him!—and when poor sweet it wasn't in the least his fault! goodness, all he'd ever said about her was why did I think her bosom made *him* melt, and once we were all at that beach and he said it soothed him to gaze down Amy's curves to the sea. Or no, down her parabolas. So do I just want you more than I did him? Because oh Charles that sounds so *belittling* as well as unfaithful!" she ended, as if despairing, and sank down once again into his arms.

This time then they lay there, it could have been, musing.

But presently, from her private darkness, ". . . Darling tell me something?—even," she asked, "if it's just a nagging little curiosity? which is what it is, not jealousy. But Amy's crush on Alec made me think of it, because at our New Year's party that lovely little menace Mimi was at one point adoring you prac-

tically in *public* Charles, so has she ever waved herself as lan-
guishingly at you since? Of course you can't possibly I know
think about her. Only of course you could, *incest* I mean aside!
But, well, one of the nights Amy was off on that publishers' trip,
ten days ago, when I rang up Mimi was *there* not in Princeton,
and right there beside you because she just handed you the
phone."

Ah, well, he said, amused, if she wanted the reprehensible
fact, the child was sitting on his bed in nothing but a chastely
draped sortie de bain, very engagingly trying to seduce him. Had
come in of course about a term-paper—some sociological claptrap
on differences, by lustra, between among others her Princeton era
and his. A boy in her class for example had made himself ridiculous—ridiculous she meant in their own present peer-context—
by tagging hopefully around after his freshman-English instructor till finally her husband threw him out of the house in a rage,
and one of *her* professors she'd never given the slightest encour-
agement to had one day just *grabbed* her!—so would there have
been such, well, such incompetent expectations in his time? So
naturally he'd said (with perfect solemnity) dear god she was
embarrassing him for his alma mater! had they taken to importing
professors from Yale or some such place these days? for what sad
fumbling!

"But Charles you listened to her?"

Dammit he'd been amused!—anyhow, she'd gone on, she
supposed he couldn't tell her personally, because of Amy, but
how at his college did students and faculty (or had they said it
some other way in his time) make out?

"Oh *dear!*"

Well god *yes!* So, making conversation in self-defense, he'd
said, so she hadn't been all that charmed! and she'd said, "When

he's twice my age?—hoh!" laughing. So he felt he'd better call a halt! So he'd said *he* was twice her age too, but here she was, sitting on his bed wasn't she? angelically smiling at him, at nearly one in the morning?

"Oh *Charles* how brutal!"

Ah, look, this was a highly charged young intelligence—and they come prepared! For all he knew, she'd read up on for instance 'deceased wife's sister' cases, and had a set piece ready! Or on primitive taboo, or on entail even; or *genetically* sisters fell for the same man's DNA and he for theirs? And this one had come prepared emotionally too—she'd just laughed up at him and said *my*, did he think he had to make her say poor Professor Staling didn't attract her but *he* very much *did*? and simply anyhow was there any reason she couldn't come put in a bid for if and when? . . . , and got up from his bed and sweetly kissed him hardly three seconds more than was sisterly, and was gone.

". . . Giggling?"

No.

"The little horror!"

Ah, now, she'd behaved.

"*Kissing* you, after that 'if and when,' was *behaving*?"

Ah, well, he conceded, no.

"But how possibly think Amy was about to give you up!"

He was silent. It was beyond fathoming. Or hypothesis. They both were silent.

But presently (by whatever contour of logic) "Does it seem to you," she wondered, "that Amy and Alec have been almost avoiding each other, I mean lately? Of course it could just be another of those poets-detest-novelists fumes they have sometimes. Or d'you think?"

He said God bless, for all anybody could tell, they were even having a sad unspoken longing for each other themselves, and were loyally fighting it off.

"Oh Charles you're *cruel,* to laugh!"

But he *sympathized!*—particularly if they were in anything like the lover's despondency *he*'d been in about her! Had she any notion of the— Well, had he ever had so much as a look from her, *or* a word or a gesture, whose lovely ambiguity could have let him hope his adoring her mattered one way or the other? Or assume he could even archaically court her? Good god, her beauty'd reduced him to Prufrock's And-how-should-I-begin! Because suppose, he'd say to himself, just hopelessly suppose—and mind you, *knowing* the supposition was neurotic fatuity!— though yes, but suppose anyway!—he'd say to himself suppose that everything, *every* perilous hope, might in *fact* (never mind any sensible likelihood) depend on the heart-stopping moment in time he'd finally risk telling her he loved her, and on the *one* right opening phrase her father's Bona Dea might smilingly decide to put on his stammering tongue to say—

"Oh *Charles!*" she cried, in complete delight, and rolling up kissed him, laughing. "You didn't *really?*—and so dejected? *Oh* what flattery!" she crooned, kissing him again.

Kind of appalling, yes, he agreed, smiling too.

"Oh my love you even made it *sound* like what remember you said once about Prufrock?—'Why did poor Mr. Eliot just out of Harvard think the mermaids wouldn't sing to him? Or was he wrong, they were just cultivatedly waiting to be asked?' But oh Charles a marauder like you dither about asking?—oh *no!*"

What was she used to—appeals to her idealism?

"Oh darling when I already admired you? No, but it's a little like something that— Well, this was a time Daddy had gone to one of those seminar things on the Coast, and he'd said come be

with him a couple of days and let him show me off to his literary
friends and enemies, so I did and we were staying in some people
he knew's house in Berkeley. But one day after lunch I'd left him
sunning in the big garden, behind, and gone up to my room to
change, an athletic poet was picking me up for tennis, so when I
heard a car come in past the house and stop at the gate into the
garden I thought it was my athlete and went to the window to
call down. But instead it was this *very* young wife of the professor
who'd organized the seminar, and what did she do but Charles
race across the garden into Daddy's arms, and then almost before
I'd realized I was astonished she was tugging him laughing back
across to her car, oh she was *dancing* almost! and as they went
past under my window I heard her say, '—and this time we've
hours!' and then they were gone. And I found all I was thinking
was oh what a *sweetie* to do that for him!—at his age to have
somebody young and pretty and adoring to make love with! and
obviously it had been going on but how had they managed? And
also I was amused—so *this* was the way women could feel about
my pa! of course I knew the way he *writes* can feel seducing, or
at least make you curious, but naturally I'd never seen a girl of
his I knew'd been making love with him, *alone* with him before.
But then I thought—and sort of soberly, my darling—but what
heavenly luck for the girl even more, for *any* girl, because how
many girls ever do? to fall in love with a man who made you feel
like that, made you feel radiant!—which don't you think perhaps," she said, and lightly fluttered his lips with a lingering
tongue, "is sort of how"—flick—"I feel about you? . . . ," and
slipping her arms under his bemused head she began to kiss him
without further analytical nonsense.

So, there being plenty of time in fact still, they went on from
there.

19

The craik and wail of gulls over the sea-meadows woke him, so early in the first faint saffron pallor of summer morning no one was he found up and about anywhere, even in this inn's vaulted kitchens only ranks of breakfast trays lined up set and ready there for this day now begun seemed to prepare for its beginning, the cool dawn stillness everywhere.

No one! He was amused.

But forbearing: so then in Finistère too, where Bretons bretonnent if anywhere, now had there been some Frankish time-motion studies?—and the efficiency of sleep!

So, like a man of forbearance, to wait, he sauntered through and out, into the forecourt's flutter of doves, white fantails tumbling in the now bronze streaks of sunrise, though at once, at the sight of him was it? an instantaneous whirr and slither about him of alighting wings.

Ah, well, he was hungry himself!

—And had nothing to feed them. He set out through the fresh green Breton-daybreak landscape toward the village and breakfast—sur le zinc as in student days, at an early bar.

Across the Place de la Mairie from which, when the librairie opened its shutters, he bought a *France-Ouest*, and a (surprising!) copy of Queneau's *Exercices de Style*, to take back, as amends if needed, to Mrs. Tench-Fenton.

Who in their room's glowing morning he found was contentedly breakfasting in bed.

And in murmuring welcome held out her arms. "But you *left* me? . . ." she reproached him, with love, putting up a smiling mouth to be kissed good morning. "I woke and darling you were *gone*," eyes smiling too. "*Heartlessly* gone," she regretted happily, patting the bed beside her with a forgiving hand (which he picked up smiling and kissed, and which she then took his wrist with, to gently tug him down). "And sweetie without even thinking what you'd left me to account for?—in of *course* came the little maid with our breakfasts, and where were you, hoh!"

'Account for'?—account for what? (he said, laughing) she think the child wasn't used to this or that offhand 'Monsieur me quitte dès l'aube' for god's sake?

"Well even if you don't you *had* hadn't you?—'d've served you right, and the child's so beautifully trained she'd simply have said, 'Oui, madame,' and not batted a modest eyelash, how *can* you suggest putting the little thing through that! At least I preserved your reputation, I said, 'Monsieur est sorti faire un tour' so would she see that his coffee was kept au chaud? so she said, 'Mais oui, madame' to that instead, darling where did you go?"

He said well these northern-summer sunrises he'd forgot how they woke you early. Brittany's latitude was after all Newfoundland's wasn't it? But *ahhh* how lovely she looked! Made-love-to lovely!—if epistemologists could contemplate her at this moment they'd renounce, forever, the doctrine that appearance and reality couldn't be the same! Anyhow, light had woken him. So he'd very quietly dressed and gone to breakfast—except would she credit it? not even a marmiton was up! the kitchen a place of shadows and silence—unheard-of! so by god he'd gone along the voie to the village for breakfast!

"You *walked?*" she cried at him, instantly appalled. "All the way into *Moëlan?* . . ."

He was astonished: this, for a mere two kilometers?

"Oh Scrope how can you *be* so devious, Moëlan's two and a *half* kilometers," she wailed, "which is five kilometers round-trip which is three *miles!*—and when to make sure you were not only properly cared for but cosseted I told them the moment we arrived 'Monsieur n'est toujours pas bien en train'? and now here you wickedly overtire yourself before the day's even begun! And especially when last night *again* you know you—we— Oh sweetie do you think I don't know what heaven it is again? but *so* soon after that dreadful not-yet-one-month-ago crisis, to talk me into letting you run *risks* because I foolishly love you and want you to be happy?—oh *Scrope!*" she rebuked him, and snatched her fingers absolutely away.

"But my lovely *thing!*" he cried, as if stricken—remorseful, even (though God bless, for what!).

"And also you *upset* me, talking French!"

So he was at sea besides. " 'French'?" he stammered. "Last *night?* . . . ?" as if scandalized.

"Well you *did!*—and totally *irrelevant* upsetting French too! 'que j'en ai le goût, de ta bouche,' you said, why *shouldn't* it upset me, the way I was feeling how lovely you are!—oh Scrope how was I *not* to think of the last time I indulged you and we made love in French, so did you mean you were remembering it too? And remembering all the other things that particular Paris week?—so of *course* in the middle of everything it distracted me! how was I to abruptly rearrange my feelings to suit you if *that* was what you stupidly wanted! Oh even with only the *edges* of my mind wondering, it distracted me! and then why were you talking about my mouth when you were kissing my throat? And then, well, I adore your mouth too, sometimes I think I'll never have enough of it, but would I say I 'have a taste for' it?—so in the middle of making love was I to be involved in *also* wondering whether the phrase had nuances for you besides what it means literally, for instance who did you learn it from?—oh sweetie I am *not* flighty and jealous and you know it, goodness! but can't you see what such *pointless* random nonsense does to the enchanting concentration you beguile me into? how *could* you!"

Ah, well.

But what endearing claptrap; so he lovingly set her damn' bed-table out of the way and took her by the shoulders. So what actually she'd *meant* was, if he ever again—

"Well you *might* don't you think have woken me and taken me along!" she denounced him.

Inflict his insomnia on her? When she was sleeping like a blissful angel? Looking about fifteen! And not really *all* that upset then anyway . . .

And kissed her. Which at least she permitted.

Because anyway dammit their French hadn't in the least upset her in that little hotel in the Rue de—

"That *grubby* little hotel in the Rue de l'Université!—and *laughing* at what you yourself called 'taking me slumming for once'!"

What slumming?—room'd had a bath!

"It was dingy and on the ground floor on the *street* and unsuitable and unseemly and even my bed-Italian was better than my bed-French then anyway!"

Peccato!

"And don't snicker! I *remember* our sweet places! And in Paris I always think about you anyway," she said sadly, kissing him. "Didn't I ever tell you about the day I got so suicidally tired of the people I was there for, the Apollinaire centenary wasn't it? anyway I got so nostalgic I decided oh damn *damn*, I'll just *go* off and touch a few bases then!—you know? where there had been something special for me?—follies too?—and, well, the Rue de l'Université darling you know *was* slummy but it was one of our real étapes emotionally, it was where you talked me out of starting a baby and I cried, besides where you said I was 'the caress of a wholly feminine sensuality,' and oh I actually went in and Scrope *asked* had by any chance a Monsieur Townshend been de passage recently, can you imagine? and they were so politely regretful at never having heard of you that I didn't even feel silly. But then I thought but supposing you *were* in Paris where would you probably be? so of course I instantly remembered that Berkeley professor's marauding little centerfold of a wife you'd not only let seduce you but she'd followed you east!"

He said dear god it wasn't just her posturing husband—he'd gathered four or five selected California-beachboy types hadn't held her interest either. But how was it *his* fault they'd fallen so short of her ladylike expectations that she'd turned to such a sad ruin of past gallantry as *he* was!

"Well but you got very fond of her didn't you? And she amused you—you told me she said things like 'When you call me *blessing* I think of church, it's confusing!' "

Damn' priests should reconsider their language.

"And you let her follow you to France too, so I remembered you said she'd found an apartment in the Boulevard Raspail near the Rue Stanislas corner, so I took a bus as far as Notre Dame des Champs. And, well, walked slowly along looking up at house numbers, wondering was it *here?* or was it *this* one, nearer the Rue Stanislas?—oh what a saddening thing, somehow, walking alone, just looking my love at *numbers* with longing—except even if I'd remembered her name *would* I have rung and asked the concierge whether she was in? oh cities *are* so sad aren't they! But finally I *did* go round the corner to that crowded little restaurant in the Rue Stanislas you'd said you and she ate at sometimes, you said it was good, and it *was*, the patronne made a place for me and I had lunch there. Afterwards I wanted to ask about you there too. But I felt too sad to," she said. "And then how was I to put it—'une jeune femme américaine d'à côté dans le quartier'? when back *then* had it perhaps even been the same patronne! So *see* what your idle misbehavior can put me through!" she accused him, happily, and took his face in her hands to kiss him. "And when I can almost even forget you for months at a time? And I *do*, almost totally, so there!—oh sweetie, forget even what you're like, imagine!"

Intermittences du coeur, yes, he conceded, smiling.

"Only then for no reason at all there will be a sort of warm flooding of my senses from nowhere (lovely!) and I wonder what *is* this!—and only *then* I suddenly realize my mind has been thinking about you to itself, and has decided I should have my attention called. So, my intermittences love, we do go on," she said, and kissed him sentimentally. "Which is why, even lovely-last-night, Scrope, I risked making you cross."

. . . about Sibylla.

"Yes, and Charles."

"But *wrangling* about it with me?" he teased her. "Lying there in my *arms* wrangling?"

"As if in any case you wouldn't *far* rather have Charles for your darling than somebody you'd have to get *used* to not detesting! Not that either of us thinks for a minute—"

God, no!—thing only too damn' clear!

"So then my old darling why *shouldn't* they live happily ever after!—once upon a time didn't *we* decide to? And haven't we? And haven't we always, even so—well you said yourself loving someone else *too* was part of the secret."

Actually, he said, it was Ovid said it. Even if he said it wrong way round.

W. M. Spackman was born in Coatesville, Pennsylvania. He is a graduate of the Friends School in Wilmington, Delaware, and of Princeton University, and he was also a Rhodes scholar at Balliol College, Oxford. He is the author of four previous novels, *Heyday* (1953), *An Armful of Warm Girl* (1978), *A Presence With Secrets* (1980), and *A Difference of Design* (1983), as well as a collection of critical essays, *On the Decay of Humanism* (1967). In 1984 he received the Howard D. Vursell Memorial Award of the American Academy and Institute of Arts and Letters for "work that merits recognition for the quality of its prose style."

A NOTE ON THE TYPE

This book was set on the Linotype in Fairfield, a type face designed by the distinguished American artist and engraver Rudolph Ruzicka (1883–1978). This type displays the sober and sane qualities of a master craftsman whose talent has long been dedicated to clarity. Rudolph Ruzicka was born in Bohemia and came to America in 1894. He designed and illustrated many books and was the creator of a considerable list of individual prints in a variety of techniques.

Composed by the Maryland Linotype Composition Company, Baltimore, Maryland.

Printed and Bound by Maple-Vail Book Group, Binghamton, New York.

Designed by Cecily Dunham.